HIDING THE TRUTH

Kristy glanced down the pool at Jazzy and Brad in their tall lifeguard chairs, then looked back at her brother. "You're guarding the kiddie pool?" she asked.

"Somebody has to guard the kiddie pool," Jonah said. "Who's more important than kids?"

"It doesn't look very hard," observed Kristy. "All the kiddies have their parents with them. I thought you were going to be saving big people."

"You'd better leave," advised Jonah, "before you make Kirk lose his focus."

When Kristy was out of sight, Kirk relaxed his shoulders.

"I think we fooled her," said Jonah.

"I hope so," said Kirk. "It'll really be embarrassing if people find out that my job is so unimportant."

"You can trust me," said Jonah. "And I bet you can trust Kristy. Your sister wouldn't blab your business to the team."

"You don't get it, Jonah," Kirk said. "Kristy is one of the people I wouldn't want to find out!"

AMERICAN GOLD SWIMMERS

SPLASH PARTY

SHARON DENNIS WYETH

BANTAM BOOKS

New York · Toronto · London · Sydney · Auckland

RL 4.5, 008–012

SPLASH PARTY

A Bantam Skylark Book / July 1996

Skylark Books is a registered trademark of Bantam Books,
a division of Bantam Doubleday Dell Publishing Group, Inc.
Registered in U.S. Patent and Trademark Office and elsewhere.

Series cover design: Madalina Stefan

ISBN 0-553-48396-X

Published simultaneously in the United States and Canada.

*Bantam Books are published by Bantam Books, a division of Bantam Doubleday Dell Publishing
Group, Inc. Its trademark, consisting of the words "Bantam Books" and the portrayal of a rooster, is
Registered in U.S. Patent and Trademark Office and in other countries. Marca Registrada. Bantam
Books, 1540 Broadway, New York, New York 10036.*

PRINTED IN THE UNITED STATES OF AMERICA

OPM   0   9   8   7   6   5   4   3   2   1

To Rose Snyder and United States Swimming
with appreciation

ONE

SPLASHDOWN!

The magazine for swimmers profiles our swimmer
of the month, KRISTY ADAMS!

NAME: Kristy Adams

AGE: 12

STROKE: Freestyle

HOMETOWN: Surfside, Florida

HEIGHT: 5'7"

FAVORITE CARBO: Fettuccine Alfredo
with lots of cheese

HERO: Janet Evans

OTHER INTERESTS: Animals

AMBITIONS: To win a gold medal in the
Olympics and to be a movie star

Kirk Adams tossed the latest issue of *Splashdown*
onto the chaise lounge, threw himself onto the
ground, and furiously began to do push-ups.

"What do you think?" his younger sister, Kristy,

asked eagerly. "I'm swimmer of the month. Isn't it exciting?"

"It's okay," Kirk grunted, sweat popping out on his forehead.

"Is that all you have to say?" Kristy demanded. She knelt down, bringing herself to eye level with her brother. "It's not every day that a person is profiled in *Splashdown* magazine."

Kirk flopped down and let out a big breath. "A few months ago you didn't like publicity," he said, grabbing a towel and wiping his face. "Remember how embarrassed you were when that reporter nicknamed us the Nuclear Adams in the article he wrote for *The Surfside Gazette?*"

"That was then," Kristy said, twirling a strand of her long, light brown hair. "If people want to write us up because we do well in swim competitions, who am I to stop them? Besides," she added with a grin, "it doesn't hurt to have your picture in a magazine if you want to be a movie star someday."

Kirk laughed. "Do you know how many people in the world want to be in the movies?"

"I might have a chance," Kristy said earnestly, "if I get a gold in the Olympics. Then everybody in the world will know me."

Kirk rolled onto his back. It was hard to believe that at one time his baby sister had been shy. "Swimming in competitions has certainly built up your confidence," he said.

"It's built up my muscles too," Kristy said, pointing her toe and proudly flexing her calf.

"You'll never have the muscles I have," Kirk boasted, throwing himself into some sit-ups.

"I guess not," Kristy said. Settling back into her lawn chair, she sniffed and smiled. The Adamses' backyard had two orange trees in blossom, and the warm afternoon air smelled wonderful. "You're turning into a human calisthenics machine," she murmured, closing her eyes. "Don't you get enough dry-land stuff at swim practice? Every day Coach Reich makes us do two hundred sit-ups."

"And I do two hundred more," Kirk panted, keeping his pace up. "Don't forget today is the first day of my job at the Takoma Club. I have to be warmed up. I may have to jump into the pool to save somebody."

"Do you really get to save lives?" Kristy asked, opening her eyes. "I thought you were a lifeguard's assistant."

"A lifeguard's assistant is practically the same thing

as a junior lifeguard," Kirk bragged, continuing his sit-ups. "A lifeguard saves lives, and that's what I'm getting paid for."

"Awesome," Kristy sighed. "And on top of that you're going to make money."

"Lots of money," Kirk said. "If I keep my job for the rest of the spring and all summer, I'll have more than enough to buy a set of free weights." He jumped up. "Two hundred!"

"You're kidding," said Kristy. "Two hundred sit-ups? That quickly?"

Kirk tensed his stomach muscles. "Go ahead," he challenged, "hit me."

"Not that again," Kristy said, rolling her eyes.

"Go ahead," Kirk said, making his stomach muscles even tighter. "My stomach is as hard as a rock. You couldn't hurt me if you tried."

Kristy got up and punched her brother in the stomach. Kirk didn't flinch.

"That's what sit-ups do for you," he said, strutting into the shade.

Kristy sat back down in her chair. "I still think you're crazy to work so hard," she said. "I just do what the coach asks me to do, and at practically every meet I get a medal."

Kirk looked down and kicked at a clump of grass.

Kristy had hit a sore spot. At one time he had been the one in the family who'd brought home most of the swim medals and trophies. The bookshelves in the Adamses' den were filled with them. But nowadays Kristy was the one who came out on top at the meets. Even though Kirk still did okay, it had been a while since he'd placed. In fact, he was barely beating his own times these days.

Dr. Kate Adams came up the driveway. She'd been walking the two family dogs, Hamlet, an old yellow Lab, and Sylvia, a lively black Portuguese water dog.

"What's cooking, you two?" Dr. Adams called, waving.

"I'm getting ready for my new job," announced Kirk.

"Wonderful, honey," said Dr. Adams. "Have you packed a snack for yourself?"

"They've got a snack bar at the club," said Kirk.

"Oh, that's right," said Dr. Adams. "Your dad and I have only been invited to the Takoma Club a couple of times."

"Takoma is a very exclusive club," Kirk said, tossing his head. "They're pretty choosy about everything."

Dr. Adams chuckled. "Especially about their lifeguards' assistants."

Kirk shrugged. "Well, I did have to go to a couple of interviews. And they're paying me a lot—"

"Look, Mom," Kristy interrupted, sticking her copy of *Splashdown* in her mother's face. "It came!"

"Your profile!" exclaimed Dr. Adams. She grabbed the magazine from Kristy and began to read it. "This is so terrific, sweetheart." She gave Kristy a big hug. "To think that you're swimmer of the month! We'll have to send your grandmother a copy of this. She'll be so proud."

"Thanks, Mom," Kristy said, flushing with pleasure.

Kirk lay down on the ground next to Hamlet and watched his mother and sister.

"This is great," Dr. Adams murmured as she read the profile.

Kristy looked over her mother's shoulder. "Do you think the picture is okay?" she asked. "My hair was kind of stringy that day."

"You'd just gotten out of the water," Dr. Adams reminded her. "When swimmers get out of the pool, they don't look like movie stars, they look like swimmers." She reached back and gave one of Kristy's shoulders a squeeze.

"The bathing suit I was wearing was kind of

small," Kristy said. "I wish I'd been wearing my new one."

"It's a wonderful profile," Dr. Adams said, handing the magazine back to Kristy, "and a wonderful picture. I can't wait until your father comes home from the college so that you can show it to him."

"Brother," Kirk said with a snort from the ground, "anybody would think Kristy had won the Olympics."

"Maybe I will someday," Kristy said.

Kirk fixed his eyes on her. "Not if you falsify information."

Kristy put her hands on her hips. "What?"

"The profile says you're five feet seven," Kirk pointed out. "That's not true."

"Yes it is," said Kristy. She looked at her mother. "Aren't I, Mom?"

"I'm not sure," said Dr. Adams. "I think at your last physical you were five feet six."

Kirk stood up and laughed. "See! You were lying about your height!"

Hamlet looked up, and Sylvia barked.

"I did not lie!" Kristy said. She glared at Kirk. "You're just jealous."

"Me, jealous?" Kirk said. "Don't be ridiculous."

"You are so jealous," said Kristy. "You wish you were swimmer of the month."

"Just because you're swimmer of the month," Kirk snapped, "doesn't mean you're a good swimmer!"

"How can you say that?" Kristy demanded. "I'm doing better than you are these days."

"Says who?" Kirk asked.

Hamlet began to howl, and Sylvia ran around in circles.

"Calm down," Dr. Adams said. "There's a very simple way to resolve this. I have a measuring tape in my office."

"Great, Mom," said Kirk. "We can find out how tall Kristy is once and for all."

Dr. Adams walked across the lawn to the converted garage where she ran her veterinarian's practice. Kirk petted Hamlet.

"You're so weird," Kristy said, catching Sylvia and hugging her. "You even got the dogs upset. Why do you care how tall I am all of a sudden?"

"It's not how tall you are," Kirk said. "It's the principle of the thing. You shouldn't lie. Even to a magazine."

"I am five feet seven," Kristy insisted.

"I'll bet you five dollars you aren't," said Kirk. "Come here. Stand next to me."

Kristy stood shoulder to shoulder with her brother.

"I'm right," he said, measuring Kristy's height against his own. "I'm five feet eight. You're definitely at least two inches shorter than me. That means you're five feet six."

"I don't know what the big deal is," Kristy said, fuming. "I've always been shorter than you are. I don't know why you have to try to make me even shorter."

Dr. Adams came back with the measuring tape. Sylvia jumped up and tried to grab it.

"Sylvia, down!" Kirk said firmly. He smirked at Kristy. "Now you'll see."

Dr. Adams held one end of the tape and gave the other end to Kirk while Kristy stood still to be measured. "Five feet seven," Dr. Adams announced.

"Ha!" Kristy smiled triumphantly. "I told you. You owe me five bucks!"

"T-That's impossible," Kirk sputtered. "Maybe it's her hair. It's a lot thicker than mine."

"Maybe she just grew," said Dr. Adams. She handed Kristy one end of the measuring tape. "And if Kristy grew," she added, "you probably did too."

"What are you doing?" Kirk asked.

"Measuring you," said Dr. Adams.

Kristy knelt down and held her end of the tape against her brother's heel while Dr. Adams pulled up on the other end.

"Five feet eight," she announced.

Kirk threw up his arms. "That's impossible!"

"It's not impossible!" said Kristy. "It's right there in black and white. Mom measured us."

"There must be a mistake," Kirk said. "How could Kristy grow while I stayed the same height?"

"Boys and girls grow at different rates," Dr. Adams said. "Kristy went through a growth spurt."

"But I'm older," Kirk argued. "I'm her big brother."

"You used to be," Kristy said teasingly. "But you're not all that big anymore."

"This is stupid," Kirk said angrily. He picked up his sports bag from under a tree. "I've got more important things to do. I've got to go to my lifeguard job."

Dr. Adams glanced at her watch. "You'd better hurry. Want me to drive you?"

"I'll take my bike," Kirk said, striding toward the driveway. "I bet there's something wrong with that measuring tape."

Kirk grabbed his bicycle from where it stood against the side of the garage and tossed his bag into the basket on the front. He bumped down the gravel driveway onto the road and took off in the direction of the Takoma Club.

"What a first-class grouch," Kristy complained.

"Maybe he's nervous about his first day on the job," said Dr. Adams. "Or maybe he feels left out because *Splashdown* only did a profile of you, instead of both of the Nuclear Adams."

"I guess," Kristy finally said. "I sometimes feel jealous when Kirk is getting all the attention. Maybe I should be nicer to him."

"Why don't you stop by the Takoma Club later on?" suggested Dr. Adams. "I'll send him a snack. The snack bar probably only has hot dogs and burgers, and Kirk doesn't like those."

"Yeah, pack him some carrot sticks and cold spaghetti," Kristy said, rolling her eyes.

Kirk sped toward his new job. The route to the club was lined with palm trees. As the wind whipped at his face, he felt himself cooling off. He was sorry he'd blown up at Kristy. Lately every little thing seemed to annoy him. Maybe that was because his performance as a swimmer was falling off. Swimming was the most important thing in the world to Kirk. The Olympics were his dream. He'd seemed to be well on the way to his goal until the month before, when his times had begun leveling. Kirk had tried not to let it get him down. His solution was to push himself even harder. On the other hand, Kristy, who had never been very serious about anything, was winning medal after medal without even seeming to try.

Kirk pedaled faster as he saw the pink-and-white gate of the Takoma Club up ahead. At least he'd gotten this great new job. Saving someone's life was about the most important thing anyone could do. And the Takoma Club had hired him to do it. Not only that, but he was going to be paid.

Skidding up to the entrance of the club, Kirk jumped off his bike. Who cared if his little sister was making more progress than he was as a swimmer and had gotten herself in *Splashdown* magazine? Kirk was doing something far more awesome than Kristy ever would. He was a lifeguard!

TWO

"Kirk Adams, reporting for duty." Kirk grinned at Mr. Baron, the manager of the pool. "I can't tell you how important this job is to me," Kirk said.

"That's great. Welcome aboard," said Mr. Baron. He was very tall and was dressed in white shorts and T-shirt. "You're just in time to clean out the kiddie pool."

Kirk looked puzzled. "O-Okay," he stammered. "Can I sit in my chair first? I've really been looking forward to that."

"Chair?" asked Mr. Baron.

"My lifeguard chair," said Kirk.

"Oh, you won't be needing one of those," the pool manager said. He pointed to a small, shallow pool. "Mainly you'll be handing out toys and straightening up."

"I don't understand," said Kirk. "I was hired to lifeguard."

"You're a lifeguard's assistant," Mr. Baron said. "You aren't qualified yet to save lives."

"But I'm an A-class swimmer," Kirk protested.

"Kirk, you've got to be sixteen before you're a lifeguard. And then you have to pass a rigorous training program," Mr. Baron said. "I thought you knew that."

"I know that's what the book says," said Kirk. "But I figured that in my case . . ." A lightbulb went on in his head. "Oh, I get it," he said hopefully. "I'm a junior lifeguard, aren't I?"

Mr. Baron shook his head. "You've got to be fifteen for that. Your job is to help the lifeguards."

"Great," Kirk said. "That's the way I remember the job description. I'll be helping the lifeguards. I'll be helping them to guard the pool and to save people's lives."

"Wrong again," said Mr. Baron. "The lifeguards do the guarding. You help out with other things so that they can keep their eyes on the pool."

"What if they take their eyes off the pool?" Kirk asked, getting more and more flustered. "Won't you need me to save someone then?"

Mr. Baron gently took Kirk by the arm and led him toward the small pool. "See all those water toys in the kiddie pool? I want you to fish those out. After that you can blow up those flotation devices and water toys in the barrel over there. There's a bicycle pump by the barrel."

"Okay," Kirk said with a sigh. "Anything else?"

"Tell the kids no running on the deck," Mr. Baron instructed. He pointed to the tiles. "It can get pretty slippery. I don't want anyone falling."

"I guess that would be pretty painful," said Kirk.

"Enforce the rules," said Mr. Baron, pointing to a sign on the fence. "No roughhousing, no running. No radios, no Rollerblades. People with hair below the ears must wear a swim cap. Now, clean up the kiddie pool. A crowd usually comes in for a before-dinner swim. I'll send over Jazzy Rubin, your boss."

"I thought you were my boss," said Kirk.

"There's a chain of command," explained Mr. Baron. "Jazzy's the junior lifeguard and your supervisor. Jazzy's supervisor is the senior lifeguard, Brad. And I'm in charge of all of you."

Kirk's face fell. "I don't guess I'm in charge of anyone."

"Cheer up," said Mr. Baron. "In every organization somebody's got to be on the bottom. Now, if you have any more questions, speak to Jazzy." He pointed across the deck to a tall, willowy brunette in a striped bathing suit.

"You mean my boss is a girl?" Kirk blurted out.

Mr. Baron leaned closer to Kirk and squinted. "I hope you don't have a problem with that. Jazzy is a first-rate junior lifeguard. You'll take your lead from her. She'll show you how to test the chlorine in the pool and show you where the mop is."

Kirk gulped. "Why do I need a mop?"

Mr. Baron pointed to the scuffs on the deck. "No matter how many times we ask them not to, people still wear their sneakers in here." He leaned toward Kirk confidentially. "It's mostly the adults," he whispered. "Some of them are worse than the children." He straightened up and smiled. "All clear? Know what to do?"

Kirk nodded.

"I'll be over in the office if you need me," Mr. Baron said, gesturing toward a small white frame building with an awning. "There's a pile of paperwork I've got to do. Some folks are shooting a commercial here this week."

"Wow! A commercial for what?" Kirk said, perking up.

"Swimsuits," Mr. Baron replied. "You'd better get busy picking up those toys." He walked to the office.

Kirk gazed at the kiddie pool. So much for his awesome job as a lifeguard. The way Mr. Baron had described his duties, the job sounded more like a janitor's or a baby-sitter's.

Kirk dropped his rolled-up towel on a chair and methodically put on his goggles. Then he stepped into the kiddie pool. The water was so shallow, it barely came up to his knees. "I can't believe this," he grumbled. He punched an inflated dinosaur and threw it over his shoulder.

"Hey, watch it!" a voice hollered.

Kirk turned around and saw Jazzy. Seeing her close up, he was blown away. Even with a scowl on her face, she looked like a supermodel in a magazine.

"Be careful with the equipment," she said. "We lose enough toys to normal wear and tear." She stared at him. "I think you can take off your goggles. The kiddie pool isn't exactly deep water."

"Right," Kirk said, whipping his goggles off. "I guess it's just a reflex. I probably look pretty stupid standing in a kiddie pool with my goggles on. I didn't mean to hurt the equipment," he added, patting the toy dinosaur nervously. He fished out a kickboard and floatie and set them carefully on the deck.

The girl knelt down. "You're funny," she said,

cracking a smile. "I'm Jazzy Rubin, the junior lifeguard."

"I'm Kirk Adams," he said with a lopsided grin. "Sorry about the dinosaur. I'm not used to picking up toys."

"Get used to it," Jazzy said, reaching around him to retrieve a plastic bucket. "The kiddie pool is a regular playground."

As Kirk climbed out of the pool, Jazzy rose to her full height. Kirk hadn't realized how tall she was. He only came up to her nose.

He swallowed. "Wow—how tall are you?"

"I stopped measuring," Jazzy said curtly. "Get back to work—unless you have any questions."

"No questions," said Kirk. "And don't worry about guarding the kiddie pool. I'll do that, since this is my station."

"Brad and I will take care of that," said Jazzy.

"Sure," said Kirk. "But just in case you take your eyes off of things for a minute, I'll be ready to jump into action."

"That won't happen," Jazzy said firmly. She pointed across the pool to another lifeguard chair where an older, red-haired boy was sitting. "Brad and I have things under control here."

Kirk narrowed his eyes and looked at the boy. "So that's the senior lifeguard?"

"Brad's the best," Jazzy said. "But I warn you, he doesn't talk."

"Is something wrong with his speech?" Kirk asked curiously.

Jazzy's face turned crimson. "Of course not. Brad is just quiet." She smiled in the older boy's direction. "I've been working here two whole weeks and he's barely said hello to me. He reminds me of an old John Wayne movie. He's the silent cowboy type." She turned her back on Kirk. "Go blow up your water toys."

Kirk wandered over to the barrel of flotation devices. He looked around, but he didn't see a pump. "Guess my lungs can handle this," he mumbled, staring at the pile of inflatable orange armbands and water toys. A woman with two toddlers in identical red, white, and blue suits walked up to him.

"I want a duckie," said one of the little boys.

"I want a duckie too," said the other one.

"You can both have a duckie," said their mother. She gave Kirk a pleading look. "Will you find us two duckies, please? Two duckies that look exactly alike?"

"I'll try," said Kirk, rummaging through the barrel. He pulled out a deflated rubber duck. "I only see one," he said apologetically, blowing air into the duck.

"They both want one," insisted the mother. "Don't you have two?"

Fishing around in the barrel again, Kirk shrugged helplessly. "I don't see another one," he said, offering the single duck.

One of the little boys grabbed the duck's head, and the other one grabbed its tail. Then they both began to cry and scream, "Gimme my duckie!"

"Now look what's happened," said the boys' mother. "I told you I needed two."

Perspiration popped out on Kirk's forehead as he reached back into the barrel. "How about a toy ostrich?" he asked.

"No!" both children screamed at once. "Duckie! Duckie!"

Suddenly Jazzy appeared at Kirk's side with an identical plastic duck in her hand. "Will this help?" she asked the mother.

"Thank you so much," the woman said in a relieved voice. She gave Kirk a dirty look. "You really should have someone stationed here who knows what he's doing." She walked away with her sons. Once they each had the toy they wanted, they stopped their crying and squabbling.

"Need some flotation devices?" Kirk called after them, holding up inflatable armbands. "I have two pairs of floaties exactly alike."

"They don't wear floaties in the kiddie pool anymore," the woman sniffed. "My kids are practically swimming."

The woman waded into the kiddie pool with her children, and the boys began to laugh and splash around with their ducks.

"Whew!" said Kirk, turning to Jazzy. "Thanks for saving my life."

"It was nothing," the older girl said with a grin. "I'm a lifeguard. And one of the advantages of a lifeguard's chair is that it has a good view. I spotted the duck on top of one of the tables."

"I'm glad you did," Kirk said, darting a look at Jazzy's big brown eyes. "I guess I don't know much about children," he admitted.

"I'm used to kids," Jazzy said. "I have a little brother at home."

"What a coincidence," Kirk said, trying to keep the conversation going. "I have a little sister."

Jazzy rolled her eyes. "Little kids are a handful."

"Definitely," Kirk said, giving her a goofy smile. "Sometimes my sister can be a real pain."

Jazzy walked back to her station, and Kirk settled down to blow up some floaties. His eyes wandered to the far end of the pool. Brad, the senior lifeguard, was sitting in the same position he'd been sitting in when Kirk had arrived. His face was deadpan, and his eyes stared straight ahead at the water. "He doesn't move, either," Kirk muttered sarcastically. "Must be some kind of statue." He blew air into the orange armband he was holding and then began to blow up the others.

In the lap lane of the adult pool, there were a couple of serious swimmers. Watching them made Kirk feel restless. The season was in full swing, and there was so much training he wanted to do. On top of the drills the coach gave him, Kirk had been doing extra work on his own, he wanted so badly to excel. Lately it didn't seem to be helping.

Tossing the last armband into the barrel, Kirk paced in front of the kiddie pool. Four more kids and their parents had joined the mother and twins with the ducks. Kirk kept his eye on the smallest child in the pool, who appeared to be about one. She was already kicking on her own, splashing over to her mother. Kirk had been an early swimmer too.

Turning his eyes toward the entrance near the office,

Kirk spotted his best friend from the swim team, Jonah Walsh. He had met Jonah at his first competition when they were both five.

"Hey!" Jonah sang out. He flashed a toothy smile at Kirk. "Thought I'd come by and say hello, since it's your first day on the job."

Kirk gave Jonah a high five. "Thanks, Walsh."

Jonah threw himself down in a chair. "Great pool," he said. "I've always wanted to join the Takoma Club, but my parents say it's too expensive."

"Mine too," said Kirk. "How'd you get in?"

"I told the manager you were my friend," Jonah explained. He reached into the bag he'd brought with him. "Want a soda?"

"Put that away," Kirk said quickly. "No glass allowed by the pool."

"Sorry," said Jonah.

"And while you're at it," Kirk said, glancing at his friend's feet, "you'd better take off your sneakers."

"You got it," Jonah said, taking off his shoes. "So, where's your lifeguard's chair?" he asked.

"They didn't have one for me," Kirk said evasively. "Actually, I'm not first in command."

"What do you mean?" Jonah asked, tucking his shoes under his chair.

Kirk blushed and glanced toward Jazzy, then

toward Brad. "They're the lifeguards. I'm just the assistant."

Jonah shrugged. "That's cool. The assistant still gets to save lives."

"Not exactly," Kirk said, picking up a kickboard from the deck.

Mr. Baron walked over, carrying a mop. "The deck could use a wipedown," he told Kirk. "Try to keep it free of puddles."

"Yes, sir," Kirk said, taking the mop.

Kirk swabbed the deck as Jonah watched him curiously.

"You might as well know," Kirk said, "I'm more like a janitor. I'm also kind of a baby-sitter," he added, nodding toward the kiddie pool.

"No kidding," said Jonah. "But you said—"

"I thought a lifeguard's assistant was the same thing as being a junior lifeguard," Kirk confessed. "I guess it was wishful thinking."

"Chill out, man," said Jonah. He reached for Kirk's goggles, which lay on the deck, and tossed them up in the air. "At least you've got a job that will last you through this summer. Plus you get to be outside. Maybe next year they'll let you do some lifeguarding."

"Maybe they will," Kirk said, brightening. "Thanks for not giving me a hard time about it. But promise you won't tell anybody else about this. Everybody on the Dolphins thinks I landed a big, important job. So does my family."

"I won't tell," Jonah promised. He picked a toy up for Kirk and threw it into the barrel. "Are you still planning to buy those free weights with the money you make?"

"As soon as I save enough," said Kirk. "When I think of those weights, I guess I can live through a little baby-sitting. And the lifeguard who's my boss seems pretty nice."

Jonah glanced up at Jazzy's chair. "You mean her?" Kirk nodded.

"She looks tall. Her legs are really long," Jonah commented.

"I know," Kirk said wistfully. "She's also pretty."

Jonah screwed his face up. "Pretty what?"

"She's pretty okay," Kirk blurted out, feeling his neck get hot. He put the mop in a corner just as Kristy and her best friend, Rosa Gonzalez, walked in.

"Oh no," groaned Kirk. "What are they doing here? If Kristy finds out I'm not really a lifeguard—"

"I'll cover for you," said Jonah.

"Hi, Kirk," Kristy said, running over. "Hi, Jonah."

"No running next to the pool," Kirk said gruffly.

"Sorry," said Kristy, looking hurt. She handed Kirk a backpack. "Mom sent over a snack for your break. All the healthy stuff you like."

"Thanks," said Kirk, keeping a straight face. He nodded at Rosa. "If you're planning to stay, you have to have bare feet."

"Sure, Kirk," said Rosa, slipping her sandals off. "We brought our suits," she added. "Kristy said maybe we could go for a swim."

"Um, you can't do that," Kirk said, shooting Jonah a nervous look.

"Can't you get us in?" Kristy asked. "Jonah's here."

"Kirk can't be distracted when he's on duty," Jonah said. "He can only have one person that he knows at a time at the pool."

"That's right," Kirk said, pulling a folding chair up to the side of the kiddie pool. "I'm on duty."

Kristy glanced down the pool at Jazzy and Brad in their tall lifeguard chairs, then looked back at her brother. "You're guarding the kiddie pool?" she asked.

"Somebody has to guard the kiddie pool," Jonah said. "Who's more important than kids?"

"Nobody," Rosa chimed in. "Guarding kids is probably the most important job in the world."

"As a matter of fact, it is," Kirk said, sticking his chest out. He cast his eyes up and down the kiddie pool.

"It doesn't look very hard," observed Kristy. "All the kiddies have their parents with them. I thought you were going to be saving big people."

"I will be," snapped Kirk. "I'm just stationed here for the moment."

"You'd better leave," advised Jonah, "before you make him lose his focus."

"Sure," said Kristy, motioning to Rosa. "We wouldn't want to disturb him."

Rosa picked up her sandals. "Bye, Kirk."

The two girls walked toward the exit.

"Catch you later," Kirk called loudly.

When the girls were out of sight, Kirk relaxed his shoulders.

"I think we fooled them," said Jonah.

"I hope so," said Kirk. "It'll really be embarrassing if people find out my job is so unimportant."

"You can trust me," said Jonah. "And I bet you can trust Kristy. Your sister wouldn't blab your business to the team."

The two little boys got out of the kiddie pool. Their mother handed Kirk the two ducks.

"You don't get it, Jonah," Kirk said, tossing the ducks back in the barrel. "Kristy is one of the people I wouldn't want to find out!"

THREE

Kirk's body tensed as he leaned forward to watch the swimmers. The event was the women's fifty-meter breaststroke. Kristy had taken her position on the diving block and was waiting motionlessly for the signal to start. The beeper blared over the speakers at poolside, and Kristy sliced into the water. Kirk's heart beat fast as he watched Kristy make an all-out effort. He could hardly believe that the powerful, sleek athlete slicing through the water in lane three was his little sister. Only a few months before, Kristy had been a novice, nervous about trying out for the middle-school team. Now she was not only one of the stars of the middle-school team, the Waves, but also one of the strongest members of the highly competitive club team, the Aquatic Dolphins.

"Wow," Jonah breathed, also keeping his eye on Kristy, "your sister might be the next Janet Evans."

"Yeah," Kirk said, watching as Kristy touched the

wall and climbed out of the water. Kirk stood and glanced sharply at the scoreboard.

"All right!" Jonah cried out, punching Kirk's arm. "Baby Kristy came in second!"

Kirk turned and smiled. The crowd was applauding. He saw his parents hug each other up in the stands. Kristy looked up and found them. Then his sister looked at him.

"Good work!" he called out, giving her the high sign. She waved at him, then turned away to talk with the official timer standing at her lane and then to Brian Reich, coach of the Dolphins.

"Wasn't Kristy great!" Rosa exclaimed, bouncing up to Kirk and Jonah with a clipboard in her hand. She was wearing a T-shirt that said I'D RATHER BE DANCING. She turned to Kirk, beaming. "She's placed in every event she's competed in today. Aren't you proud of her?"

"How do you think I feel?" Kirk said impatiently. As proud as he was of Kristy's performance, hearing other people talk about how great his sister was only reminded him of his own lackluster performances. His eyes drifted toward poolside, where other swimmers were taking their places for the next heat.

"Well, you should be proud of Kristy," Rosa continued. "If the Dolphins beat the Marlins today, the team will only have Kristy to thank."

"Kristy was fantastic as usual," Jonah agreed, staring at Rosa's T-shirt. "But how come you're here today? I thought you had jazz dance."

Rosa picked up a towel in the aisle and put it on a chair. "My class isn't until later. Besides, I love coaching, and Coach Reich asked me to help him at this meet."

Kirk turned to her and chuckled. "Come on, Rosa, you're not coaching."

"I'm the coach's assistant," she said.

"You're picking up towels," Kirk said, "and filling people's water bottles."

"I also make sure that people don't forget what events they're swimming in," Rosa said defensively, showing him the clipboard.

Kirk held up the back of his hand. "There's not much chance anybody would forget, when we write it down on our hands as we come in."

Rosa's black eyes flashed. "So sorry if you think what I do isn't important."

"That's okay, Rosa," said Jonah, glancing over her shoulder at the clipboard. "I think you do a great job as the coach's assistant."

"Thanks," Rosa said, walking away. "At least one of the boys I know on the Dolphins is polite."

"What was that all about?" said Jonah. "Rosa's your sister's best friend. I thought you two were tight."

Kirk leaned against the wall and stretched his hamstrings. "Rosa gets on my nerves," he said. "How can she claim to coach when she doesn't even swim?"

"She swims at school," said Jonah.

"And she's on the slow team," Kirk reminded him. He rummaged through a bag on the floor and pulled out his swim cap. "It just seems silly for her to call herself a coach's assistant."

"You call yourself a lifeguard's assistant," Jonah pointed out.

Kirk's face flushed. "I guess you're right. I shouldn't have snapped at her."

Kristy edged up the aisle toward the Dolphins' section with a huge blue towel thrown over her shoulders.

"Hey, Kirk," she called out, "did you bring some extra goggles?"

"What happened to yours?" Kirk asked in a grouchy voice.

"They broke," Kristy explained, walking up to her brother and Jonah. She held out the goggles she had been wearing. The plastic strap was torn in two. "I tore the strap when I was taking them off. I was so excited after that last heat I was in."

"I was excited too," Jonah told her. "You were great."

"Thanks," said Kristy. She turned to Kirk and smiled. "Was I okay?"

"I already told you that," he said. "How many times do you have to hear how great you were?"

"Excuse me," said Kristy, taking the goggles. "You'd better relax before your event. You sound totally wired."

"You're right," Kirk said, walking away. "See you guys later. I need to be alone to psych myself up."

"Sure," said Kristy. Quickly finding her sports bag on a chair, she fished out a granola bar. "Wait! Want something to eat?" she called, holding the bar in the air.

"I don't need food," Kirk called over his shoulder. "I need peace and quiet."

"Understood," Jonah said good-naturedly. "Go chill."

Kirk found a spot in the aisle a few yards away from Kristy and Jonah. His palms were sweaty, and his stomach was in knots. In just a few minutes they'd be announcing his event. Kirk shook out his arms and rolled his head. He was surprised at how nervous he was. Compared with other competitions he'd swum in, like Junior Olympics, today's competition was low-key—a dual meet with another club from the county. But Kirk had one of the worst cases of butter-flies in the stomach he'd ever experienced.

He closed his eyes and took a deep breath. Then he tried to get a mental image of himself swimming the 800-meter freestyle. It was a race that required pacing and endurance. And the freestyle was not Kirk's best stroke. Kirk's specialties were the butterfly and the backstroke.

Keeping his eyes shut tight, he tried to see himself streamlining through the air and into the water. But he couldn't get a clear picture. He was too nervous to concentrate. When an official's voice came over the loudspeaker and announced the thirteen-and-fourteen-year-old men's 800-meter freestyle, he stood up with a jolt, and his heart thudded. Snapping on his goggles, he walked to his lane and assumed the starting position.

I've got to place! he thought. *Everyone expects me to. I've got to come in at least third. . . .*

"Swimmers, take your marks." The official's voice

blared. The muscles in Kirk's back tightened, and he clenched his teeth.

Beep! The starting signal sounded, and the swimmers dived into the water.

Kirk tried to keep his mind on what he was doing. But the nervousness he'd felt before the start of the race never left him. He began to second-guess his technique and to adjust his stroke. Then, panicking when he felt himself dropping back, he swam as hard as he could. By the second half of the long race, he had no energy left. His arms felt like lead. He finished the race in fifth place, exhausted.

Breathing hard, he pulled off his goggles and climbed out of the pool. The timer gave him his time: eleven minutes and twenty-three seconds. Kirk groaned. His average time on that event in practice had been 10:32.

Murmuring a thank-you to the timer, Kirk wrote down his time on a slip of paper and took it to the coach. Coach Reich put an arm on his shoulder.

"Little tense, huh?" said the coach. He gave Kirk a kind smile.

"I was terrible," said Kirk.

"We all have our bad days," said the coach, running a hand through his thick brown hair and over his bald spot. "You pushed yourself in the beginning way too hard."

"I know," said Kirk. "It was stupid." He looked into the coach's eyes. "Sorry I let you down."

"You're not Superman," said the coach. "None of us can win every race. Go take a breather."

Kirk headed toward the section where his teammates were sitting. Then he glanced up at the stands toward his parents. He'd forgotten to wave to them at the end of his heat. He tried to catch their eyes, but they weren't looking his way. Avoiding Kristy and Rosa, he quickly shuffled toward the spot where he'd left his things.

"Good swim," Jonah said. He was sitting on an old sleeping bag, tossing up a small brown rock that he always brought with him to meets.

"You've got to be kidding," Kirk snorted, going for his water bottle.

"You were greased lightning the first lap," Jonah said.

"Right," said Kirk. "And then I died." He watched Jonah toss the rock into the air. "Maybe I should borrow your good-luck rock," he said, shaking his head.

Jonah grinned. "Anytime. I'm sure my dad

wouldn't mind. He's the one who gave it to me, when I learned how to swim at my grandparents' farm in West Virginia." He put the rock in his bag and pulled out an asthma inhaler. "See you. I've got to get ready."

"Good luck," Kirk said as his friend walked away.

Kirk slumped down onto his sleeping bag. Jonah always seemed to be in a good mood. A few months before, Kirk had been feeling pretty good too. At nearly every meet he'd won a medal or trophy. But now he felt like a loser.

"Paging Kristy Adams! Paging Kristy Adams!" Rosa wandered through the girls' locker room, calling for her friend. The meet was over.

"Oh, it's you," Kristy said, popping out of a shower stall, wrapped in a towel. "What's all this paging stuff?"

Rosa giggled. "Just trying to sound official. Somebody's outside and wants to see you."

"Who?" Kristy asked. She jumped into her bright orange Jams and pulled on an old Dolphins T-shirt. "I hope it's not a reporter," she said, glancing at her bedraggled-looking hair in the mirror.

"I don't think so," said Rosa. "This lady is too

gorgeous for a reporter. She looks like a model. And she has that girl from the pool with her. The one we saw sitting in a lifeguard chair."

"The tall one?" Kristy said. She rolled up her swimsuit and towels and stuffed them into her bag. "I wonder why she wants to see me."

Outside in the lobby, Mr. and Dr. Adams were waiting. Not far away, Kirk sat on the edge of a table, chugging down a bottle of orange juice. Off to one side stood a beautiful blond woman and Jazzy.

"There she is," whispered Rosa, pointing at the woman.

"Okay," said Kristy. "But I've got to say hi to my parents."

Before she could speak, Dr. Adams was hugging her. "Good job today."

"I should say so," Kristy's father said, giving her a peck on the cheek. "You're my little mermaid."

"Dad, please," Kristy said, choking. "Don't be so mushy."

Jazzy and the woman walked toward the group.

"You're Kirk's sister, aren't you?" said Jazzy.

"Yes," Kristy answered, smiling. "Are you looking for Kirk? He's over there."

"I saw him," Jazzy said. She glanced quickly in Kirk's direction, but Kirk pretended not to notice her. "It's not Kirk we're looking for," Jazzy said, turning to Kristy again. The tall blond woman came closer. "This is my aunt Jean," Jazzy explained.

"Jean Crane," the woman said, extending her hand.

"Hi," said Kristy, feeling awkward. "These are my parents."

Her mother and father shook hands with the woman as well. "Nice to meet you," said Dr. Adams.

"And who is this?" Mr. Adams asked, smiling at Jazzy.

"Jazzy Rubins," she replied.

"She works at the pool where Kirk is a lifeguard," Kristy explained.

Jazzy lifted an eyebrow. "Where *who* is a lifeguard?"

"Kirk," said Mr. Adams. "How is he doing? He's so modest. He wouldn't tell us if he saved any lives."

"Oh, Kirk's doing a great job," Jazzy said, lowering her eyes.

"But it's Kristy we're interested in," Jazzy's aunt said. "You see, I'm a producer. I'm making a swimsuit commercial. We're using the Takoma Club as a location. When I saw Kristy today, I thought she'd be perfect."

"A commercial!" Kristy exclaimed. "You mean I'd be on television?"

"It's going to be neat," said Jazzy. "All we have to do is swim and dive."

"Are you going to be in it too?" Kristy asked.

"I've managed to line up my niece," Jazzy's aunt said, smiling.

Kristy felt someone nudging her back. She looked over her shoulder and saw Rosa, who had been standing quietly, listening to the conversation.

"Do you need anybody else?" Kristy said, pulling Rosa closer. "I have a friend."

"Wonderful," Jean Crane said, beaming.

"I don't think I could do it," Rosa said, blushing. "My dive is terrible."

"Maybe you can be an extra," said the producer. "I'll get your number from Kristy and be in touch. Then I'll mail the parents all the details so you can decide if you want to do it."

"Thank you," Dr. Adams said. "We look forward to hearing from you."

Jazzy smiled and waved at Kristy and Rosa. "Bye. I hope to see you."

"What was that all about?" Kirk asked, slinking over.

"We're going to be in a swimsuit commercial!" squealed Kristy.

"I'm so excited!" Rosa said, clapping her hands. She and Kristy hugged. "Thanks so much for recommending me. You're a true friend."

"Did you recommend me?" asked Kirk.

"No," said Kristy. "I forgot."

"Thanks a lot," said Kirk.

"Well, you were standing right over there," said Kristy. "If they wanted to use you, they would have asked."

"You're probably going to be in it anyway," Rosa assured Kirk. "They're shooting at the Takoma Club."

"Rosa's right," said Kristy. "Jazzy is going to be in it. The producer will probably want to use all the lifeguards."

Kirk swallowed. "When is all this going to happen?"

"We don't know the details," Dr. Adams said, looking around at the empty lobby. "I think it's time we went home, though. I have early-evening office hours."

"And I've got a class to teach at the college," said Mr. Adams. He turned to Rosa. "Need a ride?"

"No thanks," said Rosa. "My mom will be outside waiting."

Kirk turned and began to walk away quickly.

"Where are you going?" called Kristy.

"Where do you think?" he said gruffly. "To the car. I'm sick and tired of all this talking."

"See you later," Rosa called after him. "I hope you don't feel too bad about your race."

"I'd almost forgotten about it," Kirk grumbled, "until you reminded me." He swung out through the double doors leading to the parking lot.

"What a grouch," Kristy complained, following Kirk out with her parents.

"Be nice," said Dr. Adams. "Today wasn't his day."

"It's more than that," said Mr. Adams, wrinkling his brow. "Something's eating Kirk. I wish I knew what it was."

FOUR

A week later, when Kirk reported for work, a film crew was setting up cameras on the deck of the pool.

"Today's the big day," Mr. Baron said, grabbing Kirk by the arm. "I want you to check out the changing rooms. Make sure the floors are clean and that there are enough paper towels. The actors will be using the rooms."

"Can't Jazzy do that?" asked Kirk.

"Jazzy's in the commercial," Mr. Baron pointed out. "And since we've closed the pool to the public, I've given Brad the day off. Now hop to it. Make sure you knock on the doors first." He shoved a broom into Kirk's hands. "I want everything to be perfect for this commercial."

"Yes, sir," said Kirk, walking out to the pool. He stood in one spot, holding the broom. At the other end of the deck, where the cameras were being placed, he spotted Jazzy's aunt Jean, the producer. Glancing around at the deck near the kiddie pool, Kirk bent down and picked up a dead leaf. Spending a day on the set of a commercial that everyone was in but him was the least exciting thing he could think of to do. But Mr. Baron had asked him to report to work, to help out. Not only that, but today was Kirk's payday, and he didn't want to miss that. Kirk only hoped that Jazzy wouldn't say anything to Kristy that would let his sister know he wasn't a real lifeguard.

Across the deck, two men were hauling in a big table. Kirk saw the producer pointing his way, and the men carried the table in his direction. Kirk smiled and tensed his triceps. Maybe at the last minute the producer had decided to use him. But Jean Crane sailed past Kirk without even speaking.

"Put the doughnut table here," she instructed the two men. "That way it won't be in the shot." Kirk watched her breeze past him again and felt deflated.

Mr. Baron came up and tapped him on the shoulder. "Checked the changing rooms?" he asked.

"Right away, sir," Kirk said, jogging over to the two white frame buildings next to the office. He opened the door to the men's room and quickly took out an extra roll of towels from the closet and put it near the sink. The floor didn't need sweeping. He dashed outside and absentmindedly pulled open the door of the women's room.

"What are you doing in here?" Jazzy shouted. She'd stuck one of her feet in the sink and was shaving her leg. "Haven't you ever heard of knocking?"

"Hi, Kirk," Rosa said with a giggle. She and Kristy were in their new swimsuits in front of the mirror.

"Hi, Kirk," said Kristy, waving with a brush in her hand.

Not knowing quite what to do, Kirk tossed in a roll of paper towels. "Sorry, I . . . didn't know you were shaving your . . . I didn't know you were in here," he said, backing out.

"See you later," called Rosa.

"Call us when they bring the doughnuts," yelled Kristy.

Kirk slammed down his broom and stalked toward the office. He'd had enough for one day.

"Did you see the breakfast spread the production crew brought in?" Mr. Baron asked, slurping a cup of coffee. He pointed outside. "Get yourself something to eat, Kirk. Before we get too busy."

"No thanks," said Kirk. "I'm wondering if I can go home."

"I need you," said Mr. Baron.

"But I'm not in the commercial," Kirk said. "Listen, Mr. Baron, this is the middle of an important swim season for me. I've got a lot of things to do."

"You can leave in plenty of time for practice," said Mr. Baron. "I want you to stay. Things should be interesting."

"I don't find watching my sister and her friend parading around in front of cameras very interesting," said Kirk. "Would you please give me my paycheck? The pool is closed today."

"But it's still a work day for us," Mr. Baron pointed out. "And I need you."

"To do what?" asked Kirk.

"To be a kiddie wrangler," said the producer, leading Kirk back outside. He pointed to a small boy in swim trunks who was standing in front of the doughnut table. "He's an extra in the commercial," Mr. Baron explained to Kirk. "I told the producer you'd keep an eye on him."

Kirk clenched his jaw to keep from exploding. It was bad enough being given the floatie station when the pool was open. Now Mr. Baron was treating him like an honest-to-goodness baby-sitter.

"Do this for me, Kirk," said his boss. "I know it's a bore. But this commercial is important to me. Besides," he added, walking up to the little boy, "Laurence is a good kid."

At the sound of his name, the boy turned around.

He had dark hair and big brown eyes, and he was stuffing a chocolate doughnut in his mouth.

"Who are you?" he asked Kirk with his mouth full.

Kirk couldn't help smiling. "I'm a baby wrangler," he said.

"I'm four years old," said Laurence. "I don't need a baby hanger."

"I'll leave you two together," said Mr. Baron.

Kirk sat down on a chair, and Laurence sat next to him. "I can swim," the little boy said, wiping his hands on his trunks.

"So can I," Kirk said. He paused for a moment. "I'm a lifeguard. Or almost."

"My sister is a lifeguard too," Laurence said, batting his eyes.

"She is?" said Kirk. "What's her name?"

"Jazzy," said Laurence.

At that moment Jazzy, Rosa, and Kristy ran out of the changing room.

"I see you met my little brother," Jazzy said, stopping next to Kirk. Kirk looked up at the older girl. She was wearing a bright yellow suit, and her shiny hair was twisted into a long braid.

"You look pretty good," he said, feeling awkward.

Jazzy blushed. "Thanks," she said. "This line of bathing suits is pretty neat."

"What do you think of mine?" asked Kristy, modeling a blue-and-white-striped two-piece.

"It's nice," Kirk said, finding it hard to tear his eyes away from Jazzy's smiling face.

"Too bad you can't be in the commercial, Kirk," Rosa said, interrupting his thoughts. Kirk looked at her. The suit she'd been given to wear was pink with flowers.

"Uh . . . what did you say?" he asked.

"She said we're very glad that boys aren't allowed in this commercial," Kristy said with a twinkle in her eye.

"I'm a boy," piped up Laurence.

"That's right," said Kirk. "How come Laurence can be in it and I can't?"

"Because my aunt only wants cute little boys in the background," Jazzy said teasingly, slipping a doughnut off the table, "not cute big boys."

"You think Kirk's cute?" squealed Kristy. "Eeww!"

Kirk felt his face getting hot.

"I didn't mean it like that," Jazzy said casually. She took Laurence's hand and gave it to Kirk. "Please keep a good eye on him," she said. "The director won't need him right away. And he can't swim in deep water yet."

"Yes I can," Laurence boasted.

"You'll be able to very soon," Jazzy said, rubbing her little brother's head.

"Maybe I can give you some pointers in the kiddie pool," Kirk told Laurence.

"You'd better not," warned Jazzy. "I don't think Aunt Jean wants him to get his swim trunks wet."

"Don't worry about a thing," said Kirk. "Laurence and I are going to be real buddies."

"He's a baby hanger," Laurence said, smiling up at Kirk.

The girls giggled.

"He's so cute," said Rosa.

"He's a lifeguard, too," the little boy said, holding on to Kirk's hand.

Kirk glanced sheepishly at Jazzy.

"That's right," said Jazzy. "Today Kirk is your own personal lifeguard. So you'd better do everything he says."

Kirk straightened up and beamed.

Jazzy's aunt walked over. "The director is ready for you and Kristy," she said, putting an arm on Jazzy's shoulder. "I'll let you know when we need you and Laurence," she said to Rosa.

Kristy and Jazzy walked away toward the cameras, leaving Kirk with Rosa and Laurence.

"I think that producer thinks I'm poison," Kirk complained, grabbing a doughnut.

Rosa sighed and picked out a pastry. "I think she's really stupid not to put you in the commercial. You're one of the best swimmers in the world."

"Thanks," Kirk said appreciatively. "But lately I don't feel like I am. Besides, this isn't a serious swimming commercial. It's more like a splash party. And anyway, it's for girls' suits."

"I wouldn't be so sure about the commercial not looking serious, though," said Rosa. She pointed across the pool. "Look."

Turning just in time to hear someone yell, "Action!", Kirk saw Jazzy leap into the air and dive into the water for the camera. Then the long-legged brunette swam the length of the pool and climbed out, smiling.

"Cut!" a voice sang out. The director came running over to Jazzy with a towel. "Beautiful, darling!" Kirk heard the man cry. "Just beautiful!" He pointed to Kristy. "You next."

"Wow. I hope Jazzy works here next year when I'm a real lifeguard," said Kirk, watching Jazzy.

Rosa's eyes narrowed. "You're not a real lifeguard?"

Kirk hit his forehead. "I can't believe I said that! Don't tell Kristy. My job is still very important."

"Why do you hope Jazzy still works here next year?" Rosa asked, ignoring Kirk's plea.

"Because she's incredible," Kirk said with stars in his eyes. "If only I was a little bit older."

"You're the most insensitive person I ever met," Rosa said, her eyes filling up with tears.

Kirk stood up. "What's wrong?"

"Nothing!" Rosa said, running toward the women's room.

Kirk shook his head and walked over to the pastry table. Laurence was eating another doughnut.

"I think you've had enough sweets," he told the little boy. "If you're going to be a swimmer when you grow up, you have to watch your diet. Lots of protein and carbohydrates."

"Okay," said Laurence, putting down the dough-nut. "Let's play."

"Okay," said Kirk. Taking the toddler by the hand, he led him to the barrel of toys.

"Hmmm, these are no good. Most of these are wa-ter toys. They don't want you to get wet. Here's something," Kirk said, spotting a bag of balloons on the table. "I'll teach you how to make water bal-loons."

Laurence nodded. "Okay."

Kirk led the little boy by the hand to the edge of

the kiddie pool. "First you fill the balloon up with water," he explained, kneeling down and showing Laurence how to do it. "Then, when the balloon is all filled up with water, you ambush somebody."

Laurence knelt down next to Kirk while Kirk filled the balloon. Then Kirk gave it to the little boy. Just as Kristy was walking by, Laurence took aim and threw it.

Kristy ducked out of the way with a giggle as water sprayed out of the balloon.

"Almost got me, Laurence!" she said, kneeling down beside the four-year-old. She shook out her hair. "Not that I'm not already dripping." She turned to Kirk. "Where's Rosa? The director is ready for her and Laurence. They're going to take a shot of them playing together at the side of the pool. It's going to be cute."

"I hope so," said Kirk. "Rosa ran away to the changing room, crying."

"What made her cry?" Kristy asked in alarm.

Kirk shrugged. "I'm not sure. We were just talking."

Kristy hurried to the changing room while Jazzy came over to Kirk. "Thanks for watching Laurence," Jazzy said, giving Kirk a big smile.

"No problem," said Kirk, stretching his arms out.

He looked at Jazzy's pink-painted toenails. Even her feet were beautiful! Kirk wanted to ask her out on a date that minute. But he didn't dare. After all, Jazzy was a year older than he was. If he asked her out on a date, she'd probably laugh.

"How's the commercial going?" Kirk asked the girl.

"Great," said Jazzy. "Your sister is such a good sport. The director had her take her dive six times just so he could get the right shot."

"I'm sure Kristy didn't mind," Kirk said, shuffling his feet. "She's really a hog for publicity."

"Really?" Jazzy said, pursing her lips. "For your information, I think your sister is pretty nice."

Kirk felt a sting on the back of his leg. Laurence had hit him with a water balloon.

"That's naughty, Laurence," Jazzy scolded, taking her little brother by the hand. "Where did you learn that?"

"Him," Laurence said, pointing to Kirk.

"I asked you to look after my brother," Jazzy said to Kirk, "not to teach him how to hit people."

Jazzy stalked away, holding tight to Laurence's hand, just as Kristy and Rosa bolted out of the changing room.

"Are you all right?" Kirk called out to Rosa. Rosa

gave him a dirty look, and Kristy whizzed by without speaking.

"What did I do?" Kirk muttered to himself.

The shoot went on for hours. At last Mr. Baron came out and handed Kirk his paycheck. Kirk put the check in his wallet proudly—fifty-six dollars.

"I don't see how you could stand diving in for the cameraman with a big smile all those times," Kirk said when he and Kristy were biking to the Aquatic Dolphins Club for swim practice. "You'll be too tired for practice."

Kristy kept her eyes straight ahead. "I kind of liked it. And guess what, I'm getting five hundred dollars!"

"Five hundred dollars?" said Kirk. "Just for jumping in the pool a few times? That's not fair."

"Feels fair to me," Kristy said with a grin.

"It's going to take me months to save five hundred dollars with my job at the pool," Kirk said.

"The pay scale does seem kind of strange," said Kristy. "But I guess that's showbiz."

"Well, I hope the commercial is more exciting on television than it was at the pool," Kirk said. They rode up to the entrance of the Aquatic Dolphin Club.

"By the way, why was Rosa crying?" Kirk asked, leaning his bike against the rack.

"You hurt her feelings," said Kristy. "You know she has a crush on you."

"Still?" Kirk said in disbelief. "I thought she'd gotten over that. Rosa's too young for me."

"Like Jazzy's too old for you?" said Kristy.

Kirk's face got red.

"Rosa told me how you were saying all kinds of gooey things about Jazzy," Kristy teased.

Kirk and Kristy passed the front desk. Kirk could already smell the chlorine. Thoughts of Jazzy and Rosa drifted out of his mind as he and Kristy parted and Kirk went to his locker in the men's changing room. Right then all he wanted to think about was swimming and how to get better at it. Changing quickly to his worn-out drag suit, he stashed his clothes in his locker, after checking that his wallet and paycheck were still in his shorts pocket. The fifty-six dollars he'd been paid would go a long way toward buying free weights.

"Of course it's not five hundred," Kirk muttered, slamming his locker shut. He picked up his bag and headed out to the pool, stopping first for a quick shower. Coach Reich was standing at a table by the diving board checking in team members. When he saw Kirk coming, he picked up a notebook.

"I read your log," he said, handing Kirk the note-book.

Kirk sighed. "Pretty bad, huh?"

"You keep meticulous records," the coach said, half smiling.

"I only wish my times were what they should be," Kirk said. "For weeks I haven't been close to my goal."

Coach Reich rubbed his chin. "Getting enough rest?"

"I do have this job over at Takoma," Kirk said.

"How's that working out?" asked Coach Reich.

"It's not what I thought it would be," Kirk confessed. There was no point in trying to fool Coach Reich. He knew the age requirements for lifeguarding. "I'm kind of a pool boy," said Kirk.

Coach Reich chuckled. "Mr. Baron has you mopping the floor, huh?"

"Yes," said Kirk. "It's the pits."

"A job is a job," Coach Reich said. "Do your best. You're sure to learn something."

"Okay, Coach," said Kirk. "But about my times—"

"They'll improve," said the coach. "Don't be too hard on yourself."

Kirk snapped on his swim cap and picked out his equipment—a kickboard, pull buoys, and flippers.

Then he lay down on the deck and began to do calisthenics. He heard his teammates' voices as the rest of the Dolphins filed out onto the deck. He waved at some of them between sit-ups—Jonah, Donna O'Brien, and Kristy's rival in the freestyle, Mary June Williams. Then, bringing his focus inward again, he picked up his kickboard and slipped into the water. He was determined to improve.

FIVE

A week later Kirk blinked back tears of frustration as his time lit up on the scoreboard—five minutes and six seconds. He'd been hoping to come in under five minutes.

"You came in fourth," Coach Reich pointed out, seeing the disappointment on Kirk's face.

"That's not my best," said Kirk. "I don't know what's wrong with me."

"You made an A time," the coach said. He put his hands on Kirk's shoulders and looked at him squarely. "The zone meet is coming up soon. I want you to begin tapering."

Kirk shook his head. "I can't taper now, Coach. I have to push harder than ever. With a time like five-six, what's the point of competing at zones? There's no way I'll get a medal with a time like that. Not when I'm competing against the best swimmers in the area."

"Check your motivation, Kirk," the coach advised. "That may be part of your problem."

"Don't tell me you think I'm not motivated," Kirk said. He stepped aside as the swimmers in the next heat lined up on deck. One of them was Jonah. "Nobody is more serious than I am," Kirk said, snatching up his water bottle.

"You're definitely intense," Coach Reich admitted. "I just think you need to examine what's driving you. Is it the excitement that made you choose swimming as your sport, or has it become something else? Ask yourself what you want to get out of swimming."

As Kirk walked into the stands, the coach turned his attention to the other swimmers on deck. *Maybe the coach is right,* Kirk thought, heading for the spot where he'd left his things. *Maybe my motivation is screwed up.*

Settling down next to an empty seat in the bleachers, he looked up into the stands. His parents hadn't been able to come that day. A few aisles away from him, Kristy and Donna were sitting on old sleeping bags, playing cards. Kristy had already swum two events and come in second in one.

Turning his gaze to the pool, Kirk was just in time to see Jonah hopping out of the water and onto the deck. His friend's heat was already over. Kirk had wanted to watch, but he'd been so lost in thought, he'd missed it. He looked at the scoreboard. Jonah had come in sixth, but for some reason he was smiling.

"Tough luck," Kirk said as Jonah came up the aisle.

"I swam good," Jonah countered, tucking his lucky stone and goggles into his bag and pulling out a towel.

"Were you having problems with your asthma?" Kirk asked. "Is that why you were slow?"

Jonah dried off his arms. "I wasn't slow. The four-hundred-meter fly is a stretch for me. As for my asthma, I can't use that as an excuse. I'm breathing fine today."

"You're so cool about everything," Kirk said. "When I lose, I'm ready to pound myself."

Jonah shrugged. "Who said anything about losing? For me in that event, I swam a good race."

"I wish I could say the same," said Kirk.

Jonah took a sports drink from his cooler and offered one to Kirk. "You did okay," he said. "You swam an A time. What more do you expect?"

"I expect myself to do better than that," Kirk said, taking the drink. "I have to be great."

"Says who?" Jonah grunted.

"Me," Kirk said emphatically. "I have to place. I have to set records."

Jonah whistled. "That's heavy. It's one thing to do

your best. But feeling like you always have to win, that you can't ever come up short . . . I wouldn't want to put that on myself."

"That's because you don't expect it of yourself," Kirk said, taking a swallow of his drink. "You don't think you're going to win, so it doesn't matter when you don't."

"Hold it right there," said Jonah, putting his drink down. "I never said I didn't want to win. I used to win all the time when we were little. Then everybody else got big and I stayed short. Don't know why," he said jokingly. "I ate all my spinach."

Jonah laughed. Kirk laughed along with him. But Kirk knew that what Jonah had gone through must have been hard. Kirk had almost forgotten what a star his friend had been when they were younger. He'd been the best in their age group. Though Jonah still managed to place in competitions now, he was no longer singled out the way Kirk was as a rising Olympic hopeful.

As Jonah walked down the aisle nonchalantly and began to tease Kristy and Donna, Kirk felt envious. It had been a while since he'd felt that carefree at a swim meet. He almost wished he hadn't come as far as he had as a swimmer. Maybe then he wouldn't have had so much to live up to. Maybe if his hopes hadn't been built up to go to Olympic trials, things would have been better. But Kirk *had* done well as a swimmer. He had set records and expected himself to do it again. The problem was, with the way he'd been performing lately, he just didn't know if it was possible.

When an official announced the women's 200-meter freestyle, Kirk watched his sister take her place in the middle lane. Kristy was so relaxed that when she got into starting position, she was actually smiling. Before the race even started, Kirk had a feeling she would do well. Kristy was on a winning streak. She was on her way up, while he seemed to be spiraling down. Kirk bit his lip and squinted. He had to make a decision. He was tired of being bummed out.

"It came! It came! I'm rich!" Later that day Kirk was doing pull-ups on a tree limb in the backyard. Kristy ran around the side of the house, waving an envelope.

"My check came!" she cried, spinning around on the grass.

Kirk jumped down. "How much did you get? Five hundred dollars?"

"I haven't opened it yet," said Kristy.

"What are you waiting for?" asked Kirk.

Kristy smiled. "It's my first paycheck. I guess I

wanted somebody to stand around while I open it up."

Kirk chuckled. "You mean spectators? You've been swimming in too many meets."

"You know what I mean," Kristy said, ripping the envelope open. "I just want to share the moment with somebody from my family."

Kirk smiled. "I'd be happy to share some of the money."

"Oh no you don't," Kristy said, waving him away. She took the thin blue check out of the envelope and read it. She gasped. "It *is* five hundred dollars!"

Kirk crowded next to her so that he could see. Sure enough, the check was made out for $500, to Kristy Adams.

"Congratulations," Kirk said coolly. He knew it was wrong to be jealous, but he couldn't help it. "That just shows you how messed up the world is," he commented. "You got five hundred dollars for jumping off the diving board a couple of times in front of a camera. I do an important job, and Mr. Baron pays me a pittance."

"Those are the breaks," Kristy said with a giggle. She kissed the check and put it back in the envelope. Turning away, Kirk picked up a lawn chair in each hand and raised them over his head.

"Don't tell me you're so jealous you're going to trash the chairs," said Kristy.

"Of course I'm not going to trash them," Kirk said, lowering the chairs slowly and lifting them again. "I'm lifting weights with them."

Kristy looked at her brother. His hair was still mashed down from his swim cap, and the back of his neck was sunburned.

"Why don't you give your calisthenics a break?" Kristy suggested. "Didn't you get enough exercise at the swim meet?"

"Maybe you're right," Kirk said. He put the chairs down abruptly. "Maybe I'd better go drink a couple of quarts of milk. That way my bones will grow faster. I've got to do something."

"Why are you worried about your bones all of a sudden?" asked Kristy.

"Taller people have an advantage," Kirk snapped. "Or have you forgotten?"

"I can't believe the way you're acting," Kristy said, plopping down in one of the chairs and facing her brother. "When I first started swimming, you were always telling me not to give up. Whatever happened to your 'try, try again' philosophy?"

"I have tried," Kirk said. "And it hasn't done any good."

Kristy stretched out her legs and yawned. "If this is what happens to you when you're fourteen, I don't want to get any older. You're so serious."

Kirk laughed in spite of himself. "Too serious, huh?" he said, tugging Kristy's hair. "And you're too silly."

"Silly and rich," Kristy boasted, waving her check. She stood up and started toward the house. "Will you come with me to the college tonight?" she called over her shoulder. "Rosa's swimming with the Waves at a C meet."

Kirk sighed and looked off into the distance. "I don't know," he said.

"Rosa's really tried hard with the Waves this season. And she's excited about this meet. If you come, it'll mean a lot to her," said Kristy. "She admires you so much—if you know what I mean."

"Yeah, I know," said Kirk. "I wish Rosa would get over her crush. It does no good to like somebody who's not going to like you back."

"Maybe not," said Kristy, tossing her head. "But it's still fun. Actually, I think Rosa likes having a crush more than she likes you." She giggled. "If you started to like her back, the crush would be over, and she'd probably hate it."

"I'll see if I can figure that one out," Kirk said.

"Talk about fourteen, nothing is stranger than the mind of a twelve-year-old."

"Come to the meet," Kristy said. "Don't be boring."

"I'll go," said Kirk. "I'll wear something interesting so that you and Rosa won't be bored to death."

Kristy ran into the house while Kirk brought up the rear. Upstairs Kristy went into her room, and Kirk disappeared into his. Some of the things Kristy had said had really gotten to him. Especially the part about being boring. Kirk looked at himself in the mirror. He hated to admit it, but he'd actually become boring to himself. He ran his hands through his short strawberry-blond hair, and a smile spread over his face.

An hour later Kirk came out of his room, wearing sunglasses and a baseball cap pulled down to his ears. He was wearing an oversized green windbreaker, Jams, and new sneakers.

"You look cool," said Kristy, meeting him in the hall. She was wearing torn jeans and one of Mr. Adams's old shirts, and she'd fixed her hair in lots of little braids.

"You look nice too," Kirk said. "Who's going to drive us? Mom or Dad?"

"Dad," Kristy replied, peeking out of the window. "Mom's still in her office. Somebody came in with a sick armadillo."

Kirk rolled his eyes. "I can't believe the pets people have. I'm sure Mom didn't learn how to take care of armadillos in vet school."

"She's giving it a try today," said Kristy. She opened the door, and she and Kirk walked out. Mr. Adams was in the car in the driveway.

"Thanks for the ride, Dad," Kirk said. He jumped in front next to his father, while Kristy got into the back.

"No problem," said Mr. Adams. "I was going over to the college anyway. My students are rehearsing *The Tempest* tonight."

"Is that the Shakespeare play with the storm in the beginning?" asked Kristy.

"You're thinking of the right one," Mr. Adams said, nodding approvingly. "I hope you two come and see the production."

"Not me, Dad," Kirk said. Seeing his face reflected in the window, he pulled his cap down tighter. "No offense, but Shakespeare's dull."

"This particular play is actually pretty romantic," Mr. Adams said, pulling out into the road.

"Thanks, Dad," Kirk said, rolling his eyes. "Next

time I want to get into a romantic mood, I'll remember that."

"Whom is Rosa swimming against?" asked Mr. Adams.

"The Barracudas' C team," said Kristy.

"The Barracudas' C team is good," Kirk said. "But the Waves' C team is good too. I wouldn't be surprised if some of the swimmers make B times tonight."

"Which would qualify them to swim in meets with faster swimmers," Mr. Adams said.

"That's the way it works," said Kirk. "If they get B times, they can swim in B races."

"And then finally in A races, like Kirk and I do," Kristy explained.

"I remember all that stuff," said Mr. Adams. "Don't forget, I used to compete myself."

Once they were at the college, Kristy and Kirk hurried to the pool area. Since spectators weren't allowed at poolside, Kristy decided to try to catch Rosa in the women's locker room.

"Just wanted to wish you good luck," she said, giving Rosa a hug. Rosa was wearing the Waves' team suit and cap, and her feet were bare.

"I need it," said Rosa. She stuck out a hand. "Feel

my fingers," she said. "I'm so nervous, my hands are freezing."

"Try to turn your nerves into energy," Kristy said. She tugged Rosa's hand playfully. "I brought Kirk with me."

Rosa's eyes lit up. "Tell him I said hi. Maybe thinking of you guys up in the stands will make me go faster."

"Just do your best," said Kristy.

Fifteen minutes later, Kristy and Kirk watched from the stands as Rosa took her position on the starting block. She was swimming the fifty-meter freestyle.

"Go for it," Kristy whispered, keeping her fingers crossed for her friend.

"I have to hand it to her," Kirk said, keeping his eyes on Rosa. "She's really worked hard."

At the sound of the starting signal, Rosa dived into the water.

"Clean dive!" Kirk exclaimed.

"Her strokes seem much more powerful than they usually do. Look at her!" cried Kristy, standing up. "Her kick is fantastic! Come on, Rosa!" she cheered.

With one last stroke, Rosa touched the wall for a finish. She'd come in first.

"Amazing!" Kirk yelled. "Way to go, Rosa!"

Kristy jumped up and down. "She was incredible!"

Kirk looked at the scoreboard for Rosa's time—39.39 seconds. "Not bad," he said. "That might be a B time."

After the meet Kirk and Kristy met Rosa in the lobby. She was carrying a medal. Her dark, curly hair was damp and slicked back.

"You did it!" Kristy said, giving Rosa a kiss on the cheek.

Kirk stuck out his hand. "Congrats, Rosa."

"Thanks," Rosa said sheepishly. She shrugged and glanced at her friends. "I made a B time," she said. "I'm such a slowpoke. Don't ask me how I did it."

"You worked hard at practice," said Kristy.

"You stuck to it," said Kirk. "You didn't let being on the slow team bother you."

"You guys helped me too," said Rosa.

"How did we help?" asked Kristy.

"I never would have started swimming if it hadn't been for you two," Rosa explained. "You were my inspiration." She looked at Kirk and blushed. "Especially you, Kirk. I really look up to you as an example."

"Thanks," Kirk said.

"This calls for a celebration," said Kristy. She dug

into her waist pouch. "I wish I had cashed my check. I don't even have enough change on me for a soda."

"Sodas are on me," said Kirk. "I got paid, remember?"

"Thanks," said Rosa. "My mother is going to pick me up at the campus snack bar. Let's go there."

"Fine by me," said Kirk. "But first I have a surprise for you girls."

Kristy turned to her brother. "I hope it's a nice surprise," she said teasingly.

Kirk took off his cap. "Depends on which way you look at it," he said, smirking.

Rosa gasped, and Kristy screamed.

"Eeww! You shaved your head!" Kristy said.

"Like it?" Kirk asked. He smiled and smoothed his practically bald head.

Rosa giggled nervously. "It's different. What made you want to be bald?"

"I needed a change," Kirk explained, motioning the girls in the direction of the snack bar. "Besides, my new hairdo might be just what I need to give me an edge at the zone meets."

Kristy nudged Rosa and laughed. "Anything for swimming."

"Having less hair does cut down on resistance," Kirk said. "Besides, I thought it might be fun."

"I think the word you're looking for is *funny*," said Kristy.

Stopping outside the snack bar, Kirk examined his reflection in the window. "I think I did a pretty good job. Hope I didn't ruin Dad's electric shaver."

"I hope not," said Kristy. "He'll be mad enough when he sees what you did to yourself."

"At least I don't look boring," Kirk said, smiling.

"Definitely not boring," Rosa said with a giggle. "As proud as I am of the swim medal I got today, I don't think I'd shave my head for another one. However, baldness makes you look kind of distinguished."

Kirk choked. "Distinguished?"

"She means cute," said Kristy.

Rosa blushed and went into the snack bar. Kirk and Kristy followed.

"Sometimes you really shock me," Kristy said to her brother. "Do you really think being bald will make you swim better?"

"I'm not sure," said Kirk with a satisfied grin. "But I wanted to do something different. And I did."

SIX

"Wow," said Jazzy, staring at Kirk's head. "What an awesome sacrifice."

"Thanks," Kirk said, trying to sound casual. Plopping down in a chair next to the kiddie pool, he began to blow up a tiger float.

"Only very serious swimmers clip their hair that close," Jazzy said, coming closer. "Mind if I touch your head?" she asked with a trace of shyness.

"Sure," Kirk replied, not sure whether to feel pleased or startled. "I guess it would be okay. I mean, I've never had a girl touch my head before."

Jazzy touched Kirk's head gingerly. "Thanks," she said. "I just had to do that. My grandpa was bald, and I touched his head once when I was really little. I could feel his skull."

"Really?" Kirk said, checking his head for any bony spots.

"You're an interesting person," Jazzy said, climbing into her lifeguard chair. "Not too many people would sacrifice their good looks for their sport."

"Thanks a lot," said Kirk.

"Oh, don't get me wrong," Jazzy called from her chair. "I think looking ugly is cool, if it's for a good cause."

Kirk put the stopper into the tiger he'd been blowing up and stared at Jazzy dreamily. He really wanted to ask her out on a date. But he was afraid she'd laugh in his face. He was so much younger and shorter than she was. And now that he'd shaved his head, she thought he was ugly.

"Ouch!" Kirk felt a sting on the back of his head and something wet dripping down his neck. He turned around and saw Jazzy's little brother, Laurence. He was wearing red, white, and blue trunks. Jazzy's aunt, the commercial producer, was with him.

"I'm so sorry," Jean Crane said, running over to Kirk. "That was very naughty," she scolded, turning to Laurence. "Someone taught him how to make water balloons," she explained as Kirk bent down to pick up the broken blue balloon that had hit him.

"He seems to be pretty good at it," Kirk said. He smiled at the little boy. "You've got good aim, Laurence."

"You told me how to do it," said Laurence, pointing at Kirk. "You said you were supposed to ambush."

"I was just fooling around," Kirk said. "You shouldn't believe everything I tell you."

Ms. Crane got a pair of floaties out of the barrel and smiled at Kirk. "I like your new hairdo."

"It's okay," Kirk said self-consciously. "I did it for swimming."

"I gathered," Ms. Crane said, putting Laurence's floaties on his arms. "Your sister was great in the commercial. I only wish the script had called for a teenage boy. You would have been perfect."

"You think so?" asked Kirk.

"Especially with that shaved head." She made a square with her hands as if she could see Kirk's face on a TV screen. "Marvelous bones," she said. "We're always looking for new talent. Perhaps another time."

"Yeah, great," Kirk said, hardly able to contain his excitement. "Just call me up."

"Listen, I have to go in to speak with Mr. Baron for a few moments," Ms. Crane said, gently nudging Laurence toward Kirk. "Would you mind watching Laurence? I can pay you a few dollars."

"Sure," said Kirk.

"Thanks," said the producer. "I don't want to

bother Jazzy. She's too busy lifeguarding." She patted Laurence on the head. "Stay here. I'll be back. And don't take off those floaties."

Laurence stuck out his lip. "I don't like floaties."

"Do as I say," said Ms. Crane.

Settling back in his chair, Kirk let out a sigh. Laurence dumped the water toys onto the deck. Kirk was used to the baby-sitting routine. Today he was even being paid for it. He ducked as an object sailed over his head. Laurence had thrown the inflated tiger.

"Don't do that," Kirk said, wagging his finger. "That's not nice."

Laurence smiled mischievously. "I'm going to ambush you." He pulled off one of his floaties and hit Kirk in the face.

"No, no," Kirk said, getting up. "You should keep those on. That way when your aunt comes back, the two of you can go swimming."

"I can swim now," Laurence said, throwing his other floatie off. "I can swim," he declared again. "Just like Jazzy."

Hearing Laurence call her name, Jazzy waved at her little brother from the lifeguard chair. "Be a good boy, Laurence," she called.

Laurence grinned and tossed the tiger into the kiddie pool. Kirk waded into the water to get it. "You heard your sister," he said, beginning to lose his patience. "Don't throw any more things in the water."

"Okay," Laurence said, throwing his floatie in.

Kirk sighed and fished out the floatie. There were two kids in the pool with their mother.

"Maybe when your aunt comes back I can help you learn how to swim," Kirk said to Laurence as he climbed out.

Laurence stuck out his chest and threw the tiger back in. "I can already swim, I told you!"

"You're a tough little guy," Kirk said, laughing in spite of himself as he picked up the tiger once more. "But I wish you wouldn't throw any more toys in here. Tell you what, I'll give you a candy bar if you pick all the toys up and put them in that big barrel."

"Okay," Laurence said, running over to the barrel and throwing his floaties in. "I'll put everything away. Just like a good boy."

Suddenly Kirk saw a group of kids walking in. Jonah, Rosa, Kristy, and a bunch of the Dolphins, including Donna O'Brien, were there. Donna spotted Kirk right away. He was still standing in the kiddie pool.

"Hey, Kirk," Donna said teasingly as she sidled over. "Don't you think the water's a little too deep for you?"

"Yeah, watch out, buddy," Jonah said, laughing, "you might drown in there."

"Very funny," Kirk said, climbing out. "What are you guys doing here?"

"Donna's family belongs to the club," Kristy explained. "We're her guests."

"We wanted to come and see you," said Rosa.

"Well, now you've seen me," Kirk said. Forcing a smile, he motioned toward the big pool. "So, enjoy your swim."

"Thanks," said Donna. "I guess we are a little tall for the kiddie pool."

"Oh, look," Kristy said, "there's Laurence." She pointed to the kiddie pool, and Kirk whirled around. While Kirk had been talking, Laurence had climbed down the stairs and gotten into the water without Kirk's seeing.

"No, no," Kirk said, jumping in to get Laurence. "You have to wait until your aunt comes back. She didn't say you could get into the water."

"Did Laurence's aunt leave him at the pool by himself?" asked Rosa.

"She's in the office," Kirk said, lifting Laurence onto the deck. "I'm just baby-sitting."

"Baby-sitting?" said Donna. "I thought you were the lifeguard."

"I . . . I was, I mean I will be." Kirk looked at Jonah helplessly.

"How come you don't have a lifeguard chair like they do?" Kristy asked, looking over at Jazzy and Brad.

"Because I'm not a lifeguard yet," Kirk snapped. He glared at Kristy. "So go ahead and make fun of me."

Without saying another word, Kristy turned away. "Come on, guys," she said. "Let's go swimming."

"Yeah, let's go," said Jonah.

The group walked away to the deep end of the big pool and jumped in. Kirk filled a toy watering can and gave it to Laurence to play with. "Pour it on your toes," Kirk suggested. "Water on the toes feels very good." Laurence wet his toes and giggled while Kirk sat back down in his chair. At the far end of the big pool Kristy and his friends were playing water basket-ball. He was grateful that no one had made fun of him when they'd found out he wasn't a lifeguard. He had been so sure that if Kristy knew, she would rub it in.

Laurence's aunt appeared with a bathing suit on. "Thanks a lot," she told Kirk. "I took the opportunity to change after my talk with Mr. Baron." She offered Kirk a five-dollar bill.

"You don't have to pay me," Kirk said. "I only

watched Laurence for a few minutes." Laurence wad-
dled toward them, carrying a big beach ball. "I'll get
his floaties," Kirk said. "He kept taking them off."

Kirk turned toward the toy barrel just as Mr. Baron
dashed out of the office, waving some papers.

"Just one more thing, Ms. Crane," Kirk heard his
boss say as he ran up to the producer. "About the
party date—"

Kirk could only recall what happened next as if it
had played out in slow motion. As Ms. Crane turned
to Mr. Baron, Kirk turned around with the floaties.
He saw the producer and his boss talking to each
other, and the next thing that caught his eye was
Laurence tossing a beach ball into the big pool. A
split second later, bending over the edge to get the
ball, the little boy leaned too far and fell in. Without
thinking, Kirk took a running dive and went in after
him. A moment later Jazzy jumped into the pool from
her chair, just as Kirk was swimming to the side with
Laurence in his arms.

"Laurence! Laurence!" Ms. Crane cried, running
over. "Are you all right?"

Hanging on to Kirk's shoulders, Laurence began to
cry. Jazzy climbed out and helped lift her little
brother out of the pool. Jazzy's eyes were wide with

fear. "Thanks, Kirk," she murmured, giving Laurence a squeeze. "I didn't see him fall in."

Ms. Crane put her arms around the little boy. "Thank you so much!" she said to Kirk. "You saved him."

"Jazzy would have pulled him out," Kirk said, climbing out of the pool. Jazzy handed him a towel.

"I should have been keeping a better eye on Laurence," said the little boy's aunt.

"Feeling okay now, Laurence?" Mr. Baron asked, bending down.

"I'm fine," said Laurence. He smiled at Kirk. "I was almost swimming."

"Mom and Dad have tried Laurence with swimming lessons, but he's not quite there yet," Jazzy told Kirk.

"He'll get the hang of it," said Kirk, patting Laurence's head. "Won't you, buddy?" Kirk glanced over to the kiddie pool. A father with three little girls was trying to find enough floaties for all three. "I'd better get back to my station," said Kirk.

"That was a very quick response," Mr. Baron said, following Kirk over to the barrel. "I hope you'll apply for junior lifeguard here next summer."

"Sure," Kirk said, beaming. "I'll be glad to."

Kristy, Jonah, and the rest of their group walked up to Jazzy, Ms. Crane, and Laurence.

"What was all the commotion?" Jonah asked.

"Kirk just saved Laurence's life," said Jazzy.

"Wow!" said Kristy. She looked at Kirk. "My brother did that? Amazing!"

"Thanks for not making fun of me when you found out I wasn't a lifeguard," Kirk said to Kristy that evening in the backyard.

"How come you lied about it?" Kristy asked, reaching down to pet Sylvia.

Kirk rolled over in the hammock and leaned on his elbow. The late sun filtered through the orange trees and onto the family pool. "I guess I wanted you to look up to me, like you used to," he confessed. "You've been making much better progress than I have at the meets. And then you got that commercial and made five hundred dollars. Lately I haven't been feeling that important."

"Come on, Kirk," said Kristy. "You're much more athletic than I am."

"Not anymore, Kristy," said Kirk. "You've become a phenomenal swimmer in the past few months. I'm really proud of you."

"I'm proud of you, too," said Kristy.

"Because I pulled Laurence out of the pool today?" Kirk said.

"Not just because of that," said Kristy. "I'm proud of you because you're my brother."

Dr. Adams appeared at the back door of the house. "Telephone, Kirk!" she yelled.

Kirk ran into the house past his mother. Dr. Adams looked at his nearly bald head and sighed. "I hope I can get used to this new look," she said.

Kirk grinned. "Don't worry, Mom. It'll grow back."

He grabbed the telephone. "Hello?"

A girl's voice came over the wire. "Hi, Kirk. It's Jazzy."

"Uh, h-hi," Kirk stammered. He turned away from his mother. "How are you?"

"Great," said Jazzy. "I just wanted to thank you for saving my brother's life."

"I just saw him first," said Kirk.

There was a silence on the other end of the line.

"Did you call for something else?" Kirk asked.

"Yes," said Jazzy. "I wonder if you want to go see *The Tempest* tomorrow night. It's a play by Shakespeare at the college."

"I know all about it!" Kirk exclaimed. "My dad is a drama professor. He directed it. He'll drop dead of shock if I actually go. I can even get us free tickets."

"Great," said Jazzy. "I'll meet you there!"

She hung up without saying good-bye.

"Yes!" Kirk yelled, throwing his arms up.

"What is it?" asked Dr. Adams, looking at him from the stove. "You sound as if you won the lottery."

"I'm going out tomorrow night," Kirk said, putting on a cool expression for his mother.

"With whom?" asked Dr. Adams.

"Just a girl. Nobody special."

"Sounds neat," Dr. Adams said with a twinkle in her eye. "You've had quite a day. I guess it pays to be a hero."

SEVEN

The next day Kirk found it hard to quit grinning. He looked in the mirror a lot, trying on different caps. Since Jazzy seemed to both like and dislike his new haircut, he had decided to wear a cap when he met her at the theater but to take it off when they got inside. He kept hearing her voice: "I'll meet you there!"

Late in the afternoon, he took a long time in the shower. Then he took an even longer time trying to figure out what to wear. "When people go to the theater, do they dress up or down?" he asked, wandering into his parents' room in his boxers.

Dr. Adams was on the telephone. "Wear the dress shirt and tie," she suggested, putting a hand over the receiver.

Kirk went back to his room and put on the shirt and tie he normally wore to church. Then he went into the bathroom and splashed on some of Mr. Adams's cologne.

"What's that awful smell?" Kristy said, meeting Kirk in the hallway.

"Cologne," Kirk said, blushing. "I wouldn't expect you to like the way it smells. You're too young."

"I like it on Dad," Kristy said, wrinkling her nose. "But you smell like you put on the whole bottle."

"I want it to last all night," Kirk said, tugging on his jacket. "How do I look? Pretty cool, huh?"

"Not," said Kristy. "Unless you're masquerading as a dork."

"It's the only suit I have," Kirk said. "It makes me look more mature."

Kristy turned down her thumb.

"Okay," said Kirk, "what would you suggest?"

"Something like this," Kristy said, twirling around in her oversized T-shirt and cutoffs. "I'm going to the theater too, and I'm not getting dressed up."

Kirk tapped his foot. "Don't tell me you're going!"

"I'm going with Rosa and Jonah," Kristy said. "Don't worry. We won't spy on you."

"You'd better not," Kirk said. He loosened his tie. "I think you're right. These clothes are uncomfortable."

"Be yourself," Kristy advised. "After all, Jazzy may be older than you are, but she's still a kid. She's jazzy, like her name. You're not going out with some grown-up like Princess Diana."

"I'll change," Kirk said, darting into his room.

Fifteen minutes later he emerged in black jeans, a striped T-shirt, and a motorcycle cap and mirrored sunglasses that had once belonged to his father.

"How do I look now?" Kirk asked when he met Kristy downstairs.

"Cool," she said, looking at herself in Kirk's sunglasses. "Your sunglasses are the best. When Jazzy wants to fix her hair, she won't even have to go to the bathroom."

Mr. Adams drove Kristy and Kirk to the college.

"I'm thrilled that you two have decided to see the production," he said, taking a sniff and wrinkling his nose. "Are there flowers in the car?"

"That's Kirk," Kristy announced. "I hope he doesn't stink up the whole theater."

"I hope you don't mind, Dad," Kirk said, glancing at his father. "I borrowed some of your cologne."

"That's fine," said Mr. Adams. "I always splash on a little when I'm going on a date with your mother."

"It's not exactly a date—" Kirk said.

"Of course it is," Kristy cut in. "Jazzy asked you

out. So it's a date. That means she wants to go with you."

"You think so?" Kirk asked, turning around from the front seat of the car. "How would you know?"

"Why else would Jazzy ask you out?" Kristy asked. When they got to the theater, Kirk's palms were sweating. He'd been thinking about what Kristy had said. He'd never gone with anyone. While Kristy waited outside for Rosa and Jonah, Kirk waited for Jazzy inside the lobby, next to the water fountain. After giving Kirk and Kristy tickets for themselves and their friends, Mr. Adams disappeared backstage. Kirk paced for a few minutes, then took a drink at the fountain. His mouth was dry, and his knees were shaking. In fact, he was more nervous than he'd ever been in his life, even before a big swim meet. Kirk turned around and saw Jazzy walking toward him. She was wearing a short dress with big flowers on it. Kirk stood up straight to make himself look taller.

"You look so sixties," Jazzy said. She laughed and tugged on Kirk's motorcycle cap. "This must have belonged to your father. And those mirror glasses"—she giggled hysterically—"they're outrageous."

"Convenient for fixing your hair, if you don't want to go to the bathroom," Kirk said.

Jazzy laughed some more. "You're so cute, Kirk. I'm glad you could meet me here. And thanks for the ticket. I wanted this to be my treat."

"That's—uh—okay," Kirk stammered as they headed into the theater. "I mean, I'm glad too, and you're welcome."

Jazzy picked seats near the back of the theater, and she and Kirk opened their programs. "You'll never guess who's in the play," she whispered. "Brad."

"Brad?" asked Kirk.

"You know, the senior lifeguard at the pool, of course," said Jazzy. "What other Brad exists?"

"But Brad never says anything," Kirk reminded her.

Jazzy sighed. "Isn't it incredible? His focus is so amazing. When he's lifeguarding he never takes his eyes off the pool. But I guess he must talk onstage, since he's one of the actors."

"I suppose he'd have to," said Kirk.

The lights went down, and Kirk felt his shoulders tense. But after a few minutes he relaxed. Now that he and Jazzy were alone in the theater, he wondered what he should do next. He wanted to hold Jazzy's hand. He tried to work up the nerve. Jazzy leaned closer, and Kirk's heart raced. He was sure his pulse was over a hundred.

"Do you smell flowers?" Jazzy whispered. "I smelled them before out in the lobby."

"I don't smell them," Kirk whispered back.

Jazzy frowned and held her nose. "Maybe it's perfume," she said under her breath. "Somebody put too much on."

Kirk took out a handkerchief and wiped off his neck. Kristy had been right, he'd worn too much cologne. He gazed at Jazzy's profile in the dimness. With the lights low, she was even more beautiful. Inching closer, Kirk stuck out his hand and felt for Jazzy's. He gave her little finger a squeeze.

She turned to him and smiled politely. "What is it?" she whispered.

She turned away again. Her eyes were glued to the stage. "Look! There's Brad. He's one of the sailors in the shipwreck. Isn't he wonderful?" Kirk felt her hand slip out of reach.

"Yeah, wonderful," he said flatly. He turned his attention to the play, but he couldn't concentrate. During the entire first act, he felt as if he were sitting on pins and needles.

At intermission Kirk and Jazzy walked outside. "Have you ever had a crush on anyone?" the older girl asked.

"Sure," Kirk said. He looked into Jazzy's big eyes. "There's a girl I like very much, in fact."

"Who is she?" asked Jazzy.

Kirk swallowed. His moment had come. He tried to work up the nerve to tell Jazzy how he felt. He was on the verge of opening his mouth when he heard hissing and giggling. Glancing over his shoulder, he saw Kristy, Rosa, and Jonah watching him. He waved them away and then, grabbing Jazzy's arm, walked toward the theater.

"Where are we going?" Jazzy asked.

"Inside," Kirk said, dropping her arm. "If that's okay with you."

"Sure," said Jazzy. "It's cooler inside with the air-conditioning."

"So who do you have a crush on?" Jazzy asked once they were in the lobby again.

Kirk gulped. "A very nice person," he said. "She's a good swimmer."

"The guy I have a crush on is a good swimmer too," Jazzy confessed.

"You have a crush on someone too?" Kirk said. He felt himself melting inside.

"This person is so amazing," said Jazzy. "I didn't know how amazing he was until this evening."

Kirk stood taller. "Really? Is he someone I know?"

Jazzy's face dimpled into a smile. "You know him, all right. He's muscular and tall."

Kirk lifted an eyebrow. "How tall?"

"Pretty tall," she said. "Anyway, it feels so good to talk about it."

"I know how you feel," said Kirk. "I've been wanting to tell this girl how I feel for a long time too."

Jazzy's eyes sparkled. "You still haven't told me who she is."

Kirk took a deep breath.

"I'll go first," Jazzy gushed. "Then you go. The guy I have a crush on is . . ."

Kirk blushed and grinned. By now he was pretty sure that the person Jazzy was talking about was him.

"Brad," the girl blurted out.

Kirk's mouth dropped open. "Brad?"

"He's such a strong and silent type," Jazzy said. "And now I see how talented he is as an actor. Of course," she added sadly, "he doesn't know I'm alive."

"I know what you mean," Kirk murmured.

"So, who do you have a crush on?" Jazzy asked.

"Nobody you know," Kirk said.

Jazzy leaned down and kissed Kirk on the cheek. "You are so nice. That's why I asked you to meet me tonight. I just wanted to tell you that."

"Thanks," Kirk said sheepishly.

"I also wanted to say that I'm sorry I was so bossy when you first started work at the pool," Jazzy added.

Kirk shrugged. "Don't mention it. I boss people around too."

"Kristy is really lucky," Jazzy said as they walked into the theater together. "If I had an older brother, I'd want him to be just like you."

At home that night, Kristy came into Kirk's room. "So are you and Jazzy going together?" she asked. "I saw her kissing you."

"We're just friends," Kirk said. Tossing the motor-cycle cap on his bed, he felt the top of his head. "I hope this grows in soon. I miss my hair."

Kristy wandered over to the dresser and picked up one of Kirk's trophies. "I thought you had a crush on Jazzy," she said.

"I do," Kirk confessed. "But she likes someone else. Guess I'm too young for her."

"Now you know how Rosa feels," said Kristy. "When Jazzy kissed you tonight, Rosa almost died."

"Hey, I almost forgot about Rosa," Kirk said, perking up. "I may have a crush on Jazzy, but Rosa's got a crush on me. I guess it all evens out."

"I guess so," said Kristy. "Anyway, Rosa will be very happy to know that you and Jazzy aren't going

with each other. She's hoping you'll like her someday."

"Maybe someday," Kirk said casually. "But I think
I've concentrated on girls enough for a while. I've got
to concentrate on my swimming." He flexed his biceps. "Feel these muscles."

Kristy rolled her eyes. "If you weren't my brother,"
she said teasingly as she walked out of the room, "I'd
say you were very conceited."

When Kirk was ready for bed, Mr. Adams came in.
"Got a minute, son?"

"Sure, Dad."

"How did you like *The Tempest?*" Mr. Adams asked,
perching on the edge of Kirk's bed.

Kirk sprawled in the armchair. "Actually, I didn't
understand much of it," he said. "But I'm sure it was
great. I was so nervous about my date, I couldn't follow the plot."

"At least it was a romantic evening," Mr. Adams
said, smiling. "And it's nice to see you lightening up
for a change."

"I guess I was getting pretty heavy about stuff,"
Kirk said, shifting in his chair. "Maybe I needed to
have a little fun."

For some reason Kirk wasn't ready to tell his father

that his date with Jazzy hadn't worked out the way he'd hoped.

Mr. Adams stood up and leaned against Kirk's dresser. "Ready for zones next weekend?"

"Ready as I'll ever be," Kirk answered.

"Try not to worry too much, son. After all, you've been disciplined about practicing for years. And you're still putting in your time at the pool every day. Sometimes when you dwell on how well you're going to do at something, it can actually stand in your way."

"Because you feel tense?" asked Kirk.

Mr. Adams shrugged. "Something like that. I remember that when I was a professional actor, there was a moment when I had to quit worrying about whether I'd forget my lines or not, or even if the audience would like me. After all, I'd learned everything I needed to in rehearsal. I had to trust myself."

"I think I know what you mean," said Kirk. "Sometimes I surprise myself in a race and do much better than I thought I would. It's as if my body knows what to do by itself and takes over for my mind."

"Muscles have their own kind of memory," said Mr. Adams. "It's great when you give something your all.

But it's also important to relax. To allow your muscles to do what they've been trained to do."

"I hope I can do that at zones," said Kirk, stretching his arms up. "A couple of weeks ago, I was thinking about giving up swimming."

"How come?" his father asked in surprise.

"Things weren't going my way," Kirk explained. "I thought maybe I was burned out. But then the coach asked me to think about why I'd gotten into the sport in the first place."

"What conclusions did you come to?" Mr. Adams asked, rubbing his chin.

"Actually, it came to me at the kiddie pool," Kirk confessed. "Watching the little kids in the water reminded me of how excited I was when I started swimming. And the way I felt the first time you took me to watch a meet. When the starting beeper went off and I saw the swimmers jump into the pool . . . well, something happened inside me."

Mr. Adams smiled. "What happened?"

"A voice said, 'That's for me. I'm going to do that.'" Kirk stood up and shrugged. "And I did."

"You sure did," said Mr. Adams.

"I love to swim, Dad," said Kirk. "And I love the excitement of competing. That was my motivation for taking up the sport, and I have to keep that. I'd begun to swim for the awards," he confessed. "I even focused on getting more attention than Kristy. But now that I've thought about it, I see that it's important for me to get back my true motivation. I think I have it back, Dad."

Mr. Adams stood up and gave Kirk a hug. "Keep swimming, Kirk. But do it for the love of the sport. That way, whether you win or lose, you'll know you've had some fun."

EIGHT

Kirk gazed stoically at the scoreboard. It was the first night of the zone meet, and he'd just swum the 200-meter backstroke. His time was two minutes and forty-five seconds. Not even an A time.

"You'll do better next time," Coach Reich said.

Kirk barely heard the coach's encouragement. If his performance didn't improve over the next two days, he wouldn't make the cut for Junior Nationals.

"We'll see how you do in the fly tomorrow," Coach Reich said, putting a hand on Kirk's shoulder.

Kirk wanted to throw down his towel and run away. He was so angry, he felt like crying. But he controlled his feelings, nodded at the coach, and walked away.

Later on, Kirk sat in a hotel room with his parents. The meet was so far from Surfside that the team members and their families had to stay overnight. The Adams family had rented a suite with two adjoining bedrooms.

"Cheer up, son," said Mr. Adams. He gave Kirk a playful tap on the head.

Kirk looked out the window. Ordinarily he would have been hanging out with his teammates in one of their rooms. But after the race he'd swum, he didn't feel like socializing.

"It didn't work, Dad," Kirk said, turning to his father. "I tried to swim for the fun of it. I really psyched myself up. But swimming won't be any fun for me if I'm going to be average."

"Hang in there, Kirk," Mr. Adams said.

"You're just going through a rough spot," Dr. Adams said gently. "Why don't you go find Kristy? She's probably in Rosa's room. Or better still, invite Jonah over. We could call room service and order a late-night pizza."

"No thanks," said Kirk, walking into the bedroom he was sharing with Kristy. "I think I'll just chill. Good night."

"Sleep tight," said Dr. Adams.

"Don't let the bedbugs bite," said Mr. Adams.

Kirk smiled in spite of himself. His parents were trying so hard to cheer him up, they were saying good-night to him the way they used to when he was a baby. But he wasn't a baby. He was fourteen. And his parents couldn't always fix everything that went wrong the way they used to.

Kirk lay on one of the beds. Moonlight filtered into the room. Hearing the outer door of the hotel suite bang open, he rolled over and shut his eyes.

"Hey, Kirk!" Kristy cried, bursting into the room. "Did you hear about poor Jonah?"

"What about Jonah?" Kirk said, opening his eyes.

Kristy snapped on the light, and Kirk blinked. Her face looked pale. "Jonah had an asthma attack downstairs in the snack bar," she said.

"Didn't he have his inhaler?" Kirk asked.

"Yes," said Kristy, "and he used it. But he didn't get better right away. His mother and father had to drive him to the hospital."

"Wow," said Kirk, suddenly worried for his friend. He sat up in bed. "That's horrible."

"He told me to give you this," Kristy said. Reaching into the pocket of her shorts, she pulled out the dark brown stone Jonah carried to meets. "He wants you to keep it for him," Kristy said, giving the stone to Kirk.

Kirk laid Jonah's stone on the table. "I guess he doesn't want to lose it in the hospital," he said. He looked at the stone and frowned. "I hope Jonah's going to be all right."

"He'll probably be okay. I just hope he gets back for the rest of the meet," Kristy said.

"If I had to miss the rest of the meet," Kirk sighed, "I wouldn't be missing a thing. Neither would anybody else," he added, lying down again.

"Sorry you didn't make the time you wanted to in your heat today," Kristy said. She disappeared into the bathroom with her pajamas. Then Kirk heard her brushing her teeth.

"I was surprised at how badly you did," she called out over the running water. "The back is one of your best strokes."

"Not anymore," Kirk said. "I doubt if I could set a record in the dog paddle."

Kristy appeared in her pajamas. "You've got a couple more chances tomorrow," she said. "It's never over until it's over."

Kirk stared up at the ceiling. "It's over for me. I'm scratching."

"You can't scratch," said Kristy. "You haven't given the coach any notice."

"I'll call him in his room right now," Kirk said, turning to face the telephone.

"You can't do it," Kristy said, putting her hand on the phone. "Tomorrow you're swimming the hundred fly. The fly is your specialty."

"Nothing is my specialty anymore," Kirk said angrily. "Don't you see? I'm burned out as a swimmer."

"You can't be burned out," said Kristy. "You're still a kid."

"No, you're a kid," Kirk said. "Because you don't understand—I had a dream. A dream to be in the Olympics. To do that I have to make Olympic trials." He stood up and began to pace. "And in order to do that, I have to make Junior Nationals. And I'll never make Junior Nationals after today."

"Sure you will," said Kristy. "You just have to try again."

"I can't!" Kirk snapped. "I'm afraid. I don't want to fail again. I don't want to feel like a loser."

"You're so much into winning things," Kristy said. "Don't be so competitive."

"I tried thinking about the fun of the race," Kirk said. "I tried to swim for the sake of swimming and what it means to me. It didn't work out." He picked up a pillow and punched it. "I don't want to swim unless I win."

"Then you *should* quit," Kristy said. She stood up and pulled down her covers. "Go ahead, call the coach and tell him you're going to scratch."

As Kirk walked to the night table, the phone rang.

"Maybe that's the coach now," Kirk said. "Maybe he's calling to check on us." He picked up the phone. "Hello?"

"Hey, man—"

Kirk recognized Jonah's voice.

"How are you?" Kirk asked anxiously.

"I'm better," said Jonah. "My parents let me call. I'm still in the hospital. A doctor gave me a shot to help me breathe."

"When will you be back?" Kirk asked.

"I'm not sure," said Jonah. "Maybe not at all. Anyway, I won't be swimming tomorrow."

"I'll keep your lucky stone for you," Kirk promised.

"Good," said Jonah. "I wanted to say good luck, swimming in the relay."

"What relay?" asked Kirk.

"The freestyle," said Jonah. "I have to scratch tomorrow. My parents just called the coach. You have to swim for me. You're the alternate."

"I can't," Kirk said. He sat down on the bed. Kristy sat down next to him, straining to hear. "I'm scratching too," Kirk explained to his friend.

"You can't do that," Jonah said. "You're the alternate. If you don't swim, then the Dolphins have to drop out of the relay."

"But it's the freestyle," Kirk said. "I can't even swim my own strokes halfway decent. You saw what happened to me today."

Jonah paused for a moment. Kirk heard him catching his breath.

"I have to go," Jonah said, sounding tired. "My dad says to hang up now. Just do it, Kirk. Take my lucky stone."

Kirk heard the phone click in his ear. He hung up and turned to Kristy.

"He's scratching in the relay," Kirk said flatly. "I'm the alternate."

"Then it means you can't scratch tomorrow," Kristy said. "Is Jonah going to be okay?"

Kirk nodded. "I guess he figured he might not make it tomorrow, when he was having that bad asthma attack. That's why he sent me his lucky stone."

Kirk thought for a minute, then picked up the telephone. "I have to call the coach," he said. "I can't do it."

"You have to!" Kristy yelled.

"I'm not going to embarrass myself in the freestyle relay," Kirk said firmly.

"Sometimes you can be so selfish!" Kristy exclaimed. "Try thinking of somebody else for a change."

"Like who?" Kirk said.

"Like the Dolphins," Kristy said. "Ever since your times have been off, all you talk about is the awards you're not winning and the fun you aren't having. As if you're all by yourself and don't even swim for a team. The Dolphins look up to you, Kirk. And so do I. Try swimming for us for a change! Try swimming for Jonah!" She picked up a pillow and threw it. The pillow hit Kirk squarely in the face. The brother and sister froze and stared at each other.

"I'm—s-sorry," Kristy stammered. "I didn't mean to—"

"That's okay," said Kirk. He smiled and then started to laugh. "You hit me pretty hard," he said, laughing some more.

"I hope I didn't hurt you," said Kristy.

"That's all right," Kirk said, wiping a tear out of his eye. "I guess I don't have very strong muscles in my face. You looked so funny when you were screaming at me," he said, starting to laugh again. "I've never seen you so mad."

"The team means a lot to me," Kristy said.

Kirk looked at his sister. Her eyes were sincere. He took Jonah's stone off the table and touched it.

"Okay, I'll do it," said Kirk. "I guess it's time I stopped focusing so much on the 'great' Kirk Adams and thought about the team. But I can't promise we'll win with me on the relay," he added.

"Nobody can promise that," said Kristy. "Just give the team a chance to stay in. Just be there. Just swim."

Mr. and Dr. Adams appeared in the doorway of the bedroom in their bathrobes. "Are you two having a fight?" Mr. Adams asked, raising an eyebrow.

"Just talking," Kirk said, picking the pillow up off the floor.

"Get to bed," said Dr. Adams. She smoothed Kristy's covers and turned down Kirk's bed. "It's past eleven. I've asked the clerk in the lobby to give us a wake-up call at five-thirty. Coach Reich will take the team to the event site at six-thirty."

The telephone rang, and Mr. Adams answered it. Kristy climbed into bed, and Kirk headed for the bathroom.

"It's the coach," Mr. Adams called after Kirk. "He just wants you to know—"

"Jonah called me," Kirk called back. "Tell him I'll swim the relay."

"The freestyle?" Mr. Adams asked, putting a hand over the receiver.

"That's not your stroke," said Dr. Adams.

"Can't do anything about it," Kirk said from the

doorway. "I agreed to be the alternate." Turning to the sink, he stuck his toothbrush into his mouth. Then he grinned at himself in the mirror. His mood had lightened up since the laugh he'd had with Kristy. And now that he'd accepted the unexpected challenge of the freestyle relay, he found himself feeling excited. He could hardly believe that only a few minutes ago he'd been ready to scratch. *Tomorrow,* he thought, heading for bed. *Tomorrow!*

The next morning Kirk got up at five o'clock, half an hour before the wake-up call. Kristy was sound asleep. Creeping into the bathroom with his clothes, Kirk washed and shaved his arms and legs. Getting rid of body hair before an important meet often gave a swimmer a physical and psychological edge. Kirk looked at himself in the mirror. If he'd ever needed an edge, today was the day. Though he was still excited about the challenges he would face, he was already feeling butterflies.

After he'd finished in the bathroom, Kirk tiptoed back into the bedroom. Kristy was still sleeping. Kirk got his sports bag and carefully packed his team suit, sweatshirt, and goggles. Before packing his team cap, he poured a little talcum powder in it so that the cap would be easier to slip on. Then he stuffed in two towels and a water bottle and picked up his old sleeping bag. The clock said 5:20. Kristy was still asleep, and Kirk's stomach was growling. Kirk wrote her a note on a piece of hotel stationery:

Gone to breakfast. See you in the lobby. Thanks for talking me out of scratching.

He put the note down on the table next to the phone. Jonah's good-luck stone was lying there. Kirk picked it up and put it in his pocket.

After a breakfast of pancakes and orange juice, Kirk met Kristy and the rest of the Dolphins in the lobby.

"I didn't see you in the restaurant," Kirk said to his sister.

"I went to the bagel place with Donna," said Kristy. "I got your note. Mom and Dad are still asleep. They'll meet us later."

Coach Reich appeared, and the Dolphins lined up for the van ride to the event site. Only certain members were representing the team at zones. Everyone seemed to be still waking up, and the ride was quiet.

After checking in at the bullpen, Kirk went straight to the showers and then came out to the pool for the preswim. The cold water hit him in the solar plexus as he dived in. But as he swam the warm-up, he felt his muscles stretch out and relax.

"Ready for this?" Coach Reich asked as Kirk climbed out after the preswim.

"Ready," Kirk said, smiling.

Soon an early-morning crowd was buzzing in the stands. Kirk looked up and saw his mother and father. Then he settled down to wait. He felt calm but kept to himself, quietly watching the other swimmers compete. All too soon an official voice announced the hundred-meter butterfly. Kirk had been assigned to lane four. He walked up to the starting block. His nervousness was gone. He felt composed. When he assumed the starting position, he could see himself in his mind's eye. He kept his eyes on the water. Energy surged from his toes, up through his legs and arms, and into his fingertips. He smelled the chlorine. He vaguely sensed the presence of the swimmers on either side of him. The starting signal went off. He arced into the water as if he were flying. He thought of the Dolphins and then thought of nothing as his body took over and he became all motion.

Kirk climbed out at the end of the race. His arms and legs tingled. He felt free, as if something that had been holding him back wasn't there anymore. The timer at the end of his lane leaned over and told him his time: one minute, nine seconds. He'd come in second.

Kirk broke into a smile. "Thank you," he said. The timer gave him a pencil and paper, and Kirk wrote down the time.

"Something happened to you out there," Coach Reich said, coming up to him. "Something good."

"I don't know what it was," Kirk said, looking into the coach's eyes. "All of a sudden I wasn't trying too hard anymore. It was as if I found a force inside me."

"Hold on to it," the coach said, rubbing Kirk's cap.

"I will," Kirk promised. He walked to the waiting area. He still had the relay to swim. He watched Kristy compete. His sister swam the hundred-meter free in one minute and eleven seconds—a record in that event for her age group. Kirk cheered loudly.

Finally the announcer called out for the swimmers participating in the relay. Kirk stood up. Assaulted by a wave of nerves, he felt his knees buckle. He closed his eyes for a moment. Then he took a deep breath and put on his goggles. He thought of Jonah and how much he would have loved to be in the race. Jonah was good at the freestyle and a team swimmer all the way. Of all the events at the meet, the relay was the one most teams focused on and the one the crowd waited for. Reaching into his sports bag, Kirk took out Jonah's lucky stone and held it tight. The stone was smooth and warm. Kirk dropped it back into his bag, feeling a surge of new energy. Then he walked quickly to his place on the deck with the other three swimmers representing the Dolphins. The first swimmers took their positions. Kirk was the anchor—he would swim last.

The starting signal sounded, and the first swimmers dived in. The race was a series of sprints, calling for an all-out effort from each swimmer. Kirk inched forward as the first swimmer touched the wall and the second dived. The crowd became louder as the second swimmers surged forward, touched the wall, and changed directions, speeding back to touch the wall again.

The third swimmer dived in, and Kirk got into position. His body was taut and motionless. He couldn't move an instant too early or he'd be disqualified and the team would forfeit. Kirk's teammate touched the wall. In a split-second reflex, Kirk flew into the water. Though freestyle wasn't his specialty, he'd practiced it since he was four. All his technique came into play as he shot forward, touched the wall, turned, and with powerful strokes and kicks propelled himself back. As he touched the wall again, the crowd cheered. He climbed out of the water. His teammates were yelling. The scoreboard was lit up. In bright lights he saw the name of his team—*DOLPHINS!* His team had come in first! Kirk felt himself starting to cry. He tried to hide his feelings, but he couldn't.

"Let it out," said the coach, giving him a hug. "A win like this is bound to bring some emotion."

Kirk sniffed and smiled. He looked at the stands and saw Kristy and his parents. And right next to them were Mr. and Mrs. Walsh and Jonah. Kirk gave him the high sign. Jonah waved a fist in triumph. Kirk took his towel and walked toward the stands, experiencing the disbelief he always felt when a meet was over. So much preparation and anticipation went into swimming a race, so many weeks of work. And then the whole thing was over, like a dream.

But this year's zone competition was a meet Kirk would never forget, and not only because he'd made well over an A time in the hundred-meter fly and led the Dolphins to victory in the freestyle relay. In this meet, Kirk had been challenged. Having swum his worst, he'd managed to keep going to swim his best.

NINE

"Hey, Kirk! Mail!"

As her brother ambled in from the patio, Kristy ripped open a light blue envelope.

"What did you get?" Kirk asked. "Another check for five hundred dollars?"

"Not exactly," Kristy said, pulling a rectangular card out of the envelope. "It's an invitation. Addressed to both of us. The swimsuit company I did the commercial for is giving a splash party!"

Kirk rubbed his head. "A splash party, huh? I don't know. After all the competing we've been doing, I feel kind of waterlogged."

"You have to go," Kristy said, thrusting the invitation into his hand. "They're previewing the commercial that I was in with Rosa, Jazzy, and Laurence. I bet there's going to be lots of great food," she continued excitedly. "And maybe even some music. Remember those pastries the producer brought the day the commercial got shot?"

"I remember," said Kirk. "I was sitting right next to the pastry table. Jazzy's aunt wanted me out of the way so I wouldn't be in the shot."

"Haven't you gotten over that yet?" Kristy asked. "Be a good sport."

"Don't worry, I've gotten over being jealous about not being in the commercial. I've had more than my share of good luck these days," Kirk said. It was true. Ever since he'd overcome the rough patch he'd experienced before zones, he'd been swimming better than ever. He also felt a lot more relaxed—maybe because he wasn't worrying as much about winning.

"If you don't go to the party," warned Kristy, "you're going to miss out on a lot of fun. And since she was in the commercial, I'm sure Jazzy will be there." She gave Kirk a look.

Kirk chuckled. "Sure, I'll go. I wouldn't want to miss the preview of your commercial. And I guess it would be fun to see Jazzy at a party. When I see her at work, I don't get to talk to her much."

"How come?" asked Kristy. "Because you sit next to the kiddie pool and she's up in the lifeguard chair?"

Kirk shrugged. "She kind of likes the other lifeguard at the pool. The one named Brad."

"Yuck," said Kristy. "I've seen him. He doesn't

even say hello to people. You're much cuter than he is," she added earnestly.

"Thanks," said Kirk. "It's nice to know that at least one girl feels that way. Even if she is my sister."

"Make that two girls," said Kristy. "Don't forget about Rosa."

Kirk rolled his eyes. "Rosa doesn't like me. She just likes having a crush."

Kristy giggled. "It's so silly. I wouldn't be caught dead having a crush on a boy."

"Kristy! A package for you arrived!" Dr. Adams peeked out through the doors that led from the den to the patio. Sylvia and Hamlet crowded on either side of her. Sylvia was wagging her tail wildly, and Hamlet was panting.

"The dogs got excited when the delivery man came to the front door," said Dr. Adams. "There's a box out front with your name on it, Kristy. But it's kind of heavy."

"Maybe Kirk can help me bring it in," Kristy said with a twinkle in her eye.

"Sure," said Kirk, flexing one of his biceps. "I can handle it."

Kristy ran to the front door, followed by Kirk, Dr. Adams, and the two dogs. A long, flat box sat on the front porch.

Kirk shrugged and reached for it. "That doesn't look heavy at all, Mom," he said. He tried to lift the box off the ground but couldn't. "Guess it's heavier than it looks," he said. "What's in it?"

"Oh, something I sent away for," said Kristy. "Maybe we should open it out here."

"I'll get some scissors to cut through the packing tape," Dr. Adams said, running back into the living room.

"What did you buy yourself?" Kirk asked Kristy. He looked at the return address on the box. "It came from a place that sells sports equipment."

Dr. Adams appeared with the scissors, and Kristy ripped open the box.

"What do you know?" she said, peeling back the flaps on the carton. "A set of free weights."

Kirk's eyes and mouth opened wide. "Free weights! Fantastic!" Glancing at Kristy, his face fell. "You got some for yourself, huh?"

"No, silly," she said. "They're for you. I figured if I made five hundred dollars for one day's work, I should share some of it."

"All right!" yelled Kirk. He hugged his mother and Kristy and petted Sylvia and Hamlet. "Thank you, thank you, thank you!"

Kristy laughed, and the dogs began barking. Dr. Adams smiled and shook her head. "I guess we can expect your muscles to be getting bulkier," she said to Kirk. "Please don't overdo it. I'm still getting over the shock of your shaved head."

"I won't overdo," Kirk promised. "I'll just follow the program the coach gives me." Running his fingers over the weights, he looked up at Kristy. "Thanks, sis. Of all the neat things that have happened lately, I'd have to say that this is the neatest."

"Aren't you going to even bring a swimsuit?" Kristy asked. "After all, we're going to a splash party."

"I told you before," Kirk said. "I'm in the water enough between competitions and practice. I want to keep dry for a change. There's no way anyone can get me to go into a pool today."

"Too bad," Kristy said, wrinkling her nose. They turned around and waved good-bye to their parents, then walked toward the front entrance of the Takoma Club. Kristy looked at Kirk and wrinkled her nose again.

"Why do you keep wrinkling your nose like that?" Kirk asked. "Do you smell something?"

"Yes," said Kristy. "You. You put on Dad's cologne again. That's why you should go swimming. Then you could wash some of the smell off."

"I don't need to wash any off," Kirk said. "This time I put on just the right amount. The problem with you is that you're too young to appreciate something like cologne."

"And I suppose Jazzy is old enough to appreciate it?" Kristy said with a giggle.

"Who said anything about Jazzy?" Kirk said as his face got redder. "She likes Brad."

"But I guess that won't stop you from trying," Kristy teased.

As they walked through the front door of the club and down the walkway to the pool entrance, Kirk and Kristy heard loud music.

"That's one of my favorite CDs," Kristy squealed. "I guess Jazzy's aunt brought in a sound system. This is going to be some party!" She ran down the walkway.

Watching his little sister take off, Kirk stepped onto the deck of the pool and looked around. The producers of the commercial had invited Kirk and Kristy's whole swim team. Lots of the Dolphins were there. Some of them were already in the water. But more of them were hanging out on the deck in their Jams and T-shirts.

"Take those shoes off!" a voice barked. "No sneakers allowed on the deck!"

Kirk whirled around to see Jonah.

"Just doing your job for you," Kirk's friend laughed, pointing down at Kirk's shoes.

Kirk smiled and shuffled his feet. "I don't think the rules apply at a party," he said. "But if they do, I'm not enforcing them. I'm not working today."

"I see that," Jonah said, taking in Kirk's new black T-shirt and Jams. Jonah was wearing an old pair of trunks, and he looked as if he'd already been in the water. "I'll pinch-hit as lifeguard today," Jonah said jokingly, "if you put in a word for me with Mr. Baron."

"I'd be glad to," Kirk said. He clapped Jonah's shoulder. "Wouldn't it be great if this time next summer, we were both working here?"

"That would definitely be cool," said Jonah. He moved his head in time to the music. "The sounds they picked up are nice. I'm going to check out the food."

"Catch you later, buddy," said Kirk. "I'll just hang here. There's somebody I'm waiting for. By the way," he asked as Jonah walked off, "how's your asthma?"

"Under control," Jonah called over his shoulder. "As long as I've got my inhaler. The doctor told me one of the best things I could do is to keep right on swimming."

Kirk watched Jonah head for the food table and grab a slice of pizza. Lots of other team members were standing around eating as well. Kirk's stomach growled. He wanted to eat too. But before he did anything at the party, he wanted to see Jazzy. Even if Jazzy liked Brad, Kirk still had a crush on her. And seeing her at a party was a lot more special than seeing her at work.

As he gazed toward the changing rooms, Kirk saw her. She was with Laurence, and they were walking right toward him.

"Just the person I wanted to see," Jazzy said, flashing a big smile at Kirk.

"Me?" Kirk said in surprise.

"Who else?" Jazzy said. She rubbed Laurence's head and gently pushed him forward. "There he is, Laurence," she said. "You're his hero," she whispered to Kirk.

Kirk knelt down and shook Laurence's hand. "How are you, little guy?"

"I can swim," said Laurence.

"I know you can," Kirk said, standing up. "But not without your floaties."

"He can swim without them now," Jazzy said excitedly. "He wants to show you. When he found out he was coming to the party today, that's all he could talk about."

Kirk smiled and pointed to the kiddie pool. "Want to show me how you can swim, Laurence?"

"I'll get in with him," said Jazzy, who was wearing a suit. "Laurence wants you to get in too."

"Sorry," said Kirk. "I didn't bring a suit."

"Borrow one from Mr. Baron," Jazzy suggested. She batted her eyes at Kirk. "Please . . ."

"Sure," Kirk said, melting. "I think Mr. Baron has some old spares in the office somewhere."

In five minutes he was back, wearing an oversized pair of Hawaiian-print trunks.

"This is the best I could find," he said, cinching the waist tighter. "I hope they don't fall . . ." He caught himself and blushed. "You know what I mean."

"They won't," Jazzy said, stepping into the kiddie pool and helping Laurence climb in. "After all, we're not going into very deep water."

Kirk stepped into the kiddie pool and knelt down facing Jazzy. The oversized shorts ballooned in the water. He knew he probably looked silly, but it didn't matter. He liked Laurence a lot. And he certainly liked Jazzy.

"Okay, Laurence," Jazzy said. "Show Kirk your stroke."

"All right," the little boy said. "Watch." Jazzy stood in the middle of the pool, and Kirk knelt at the end. Laurence waded out to Jazzy and held his nose.

"On the count of three," Jazzy said. "Get into the water and kick and stroke."

"Swim to me," Kirk coaxed.

Jazzy counted to three, and Laurence plunged in. Kirk reached out as the little boy dog-paddled toward him, kicking his legs as hard as he could. Kirk caught his hands and pulled him out.

"Very good, Laurence," he said.

Laurence smiled and patted Kirk's face. "I told you I could swim."

Jazzy walked over and took her little brother from Kirk. "Thanks a lot," she said. "And thanks for being such a good friend."

"Sure," Kirk said, startled by the remark. "I'm your friend?"

"Of course you're my friend," Jazzy said, helping Laurence out of the pool.

Kirk gave the little boy a towel.

"You let me talk about Brad," Jazzy whispered. "You're the only one I've told."

Kirk's face fell. "Oh, right. I'd almost forgotten." He gazed down the pool at the lifeguard. "Has he said anything to you yet?"

"Nothing," said Jazzy. "Maybe he'll speak to me today. But I doubt it, since he's the official lifeguard at the party. He has to keep his eyes on everything, so he'll be too busy." She reached out and touched Kirk's hand. He felt something like an electric shock. "You just can't imagine what it's like to have a crush on someone and have them not notice you," she confided.

Kirk sighed.

"Attention, everybody!" Jazzy's aunt called out. The music stopped. "We're going to preview the commercial!" she announced. "There's a large-screen television set up in the lounge. This is only a rough cut. We still have just a bit more editing to do. But what you'll see inside should give you a good idea of how great our actors were—Kristy Adams of the Dolphins and the Surfside Waves, Rosa Gonzalez of the Surfside Waves, and Jazzy and Laurence Rubin. After the tape plays, someone will put it on rewind. So preview it when you have a chance. And thank you all for coming!"

"Want to see the commercial?" asked Jazzy.

"I wouldn't miss it," said Kirk, heading toward the lounge with the rest of the crowd. Inside, he spotted Kristy and Rosa. His sister and her friend had planted themselves six inches from the gigantic screen in the front row.

The soundtrack blared out of the speaker as the commercial flicked onto the screen. Suddenly he saw a close-up of Kristy's face, then a long shot of Jazzy in her swimsuit, then several takes of the two girls diving. A voice-over talked about the suit and how it was ideal for athletic girls. At the close there was a long shot of the pool and club buildings. In the background Rosa sat in a lounge chair with Laurence walking up to her. The very last shot was of some palm trees and a table. Then Kirk caught sight of himself for just a second.

The tape rolled to a halt, and everyone clapped. Kirk was very excited. "Can we roll that again?" he yelled. "I think I saw myself."

"You couldn't have," Jonah said, overhearing him. "You weren't in the commercial."

"Yes, I was!" Kirk exclaimed, walking up to the television. "I just saw myself," he declared. "It was only for a second. But I was there."

Rosa stood up, and so did Kristy.

"Did you see me?" asked Kirk.

"I saw myself and Rosa and Jazzy," said Kristy. "And Laurence was so cute!"

"I think I might have seen your arm," Rosa told Kirk. "At the very end."

"You see," Kirk said, turning around, "I was in it."

"Sorry about that," Jazzy's aunt said, sailing up to him. "The commercial isn't quite finished. This is just a rough cut. That very last moment you saw is an outtake."

"An outtake?" Kirk said. "What's that? Am I in the commercial too?"

"No, that little moment at the end is going to be cut," the producer explained. "It's going to be taken out. Excuse me, I have to rewind the tape."

"Sure," said Kirk.

Rosa patted Kirk's arm. "Sorry," she said. "I think you would have been great in the commercial."

"No problem," Kirk said, laughing. "When I saw myself just for a second, I thought . . . I guess I'm pretty conceited."

"No, you're not," Rosa said, looking into his eyes dreamily. "By the way, congratulations. Kristy told me all about zones. What's next? Junior Nationals?"

"I'm gearing up for it," said Kirk. "My zone times qualified me after all."

Jazzy walked over to Rosa and Kirk. "Look at

Kristy," she whispered, pointing to a corner of the lounge. Kristy was sitting at a table with a boy.

"Who's that guy she's sitting with?" asked Kirk.

"His family belongs to the club," Jazzy explained.

"He and Kristy seem to know each other," Kirk said. "They're laughing a lot together."

"They just met outside," said Rosa. "I think Kristy likes him."

"Kristy doesn't have crushes on boys," said Kirk. "She thinks it's silly."

Rosa sighed. "Maybe she's right."

"It can be silly if the person you have a crush on doesn't like you because you're too young," Kirk pointed out tactfully.

"I know what you mean," said Jazzy, gazing out the window at Brad.

Standing between the girl who liked him and the girl whom he liked, Kirk watched his sister talking to the new boy.

"Kristy definitely has a crush on him," Rosa whispered. "Look how she's smiling."

"She does look a little goofy," Kirk agreed. "We'd better keep an eye on her."

Kirk, Jazzy, and Rosa got pizza and then joined Kristy and the boy at their table. Someone put another CD on the sound system. Outside at the pool, Jonah and Donna started to dance. Everybody had on a swimsuit, though at the moment not a single swimmer was in the water. There would be plenty of time for that in the weeks ahead. The season wasn't over.

ABOUT THE AUTHOR

SHARON DENNIS WYETH has written many books for young readers, including *Vampire Bugs: Stories Conjured from the Past, The World of Daughter McGuire,* and the Pen Pals series. She lives in Montclair, New Jersey, with her husband, Sims, and daughter, Georgia.

HOW TO WATCH SWIMMING AT THE SUMMER OLYMPICS IN ATLANTA

by Rose Snyder
Age Group Program Director
at United States Swimming

The first recorded Olympics took place in Greece in 776 B.C. Swimming did not make its debut until much later, at the modern games in 1896. Since then, some true stars have swum for the United States. Johnny Weissmuller won five gold medals—and never lost a race in his career. Tracy Caulkins is the most outstanding U.S. woman swimmer. During her career, she won three golds and broke three world records. She's also the only swimmer to hold every U.S. women's record at the same time. Mark Spitz won seven gold medals at the 1972 Olympics—a feat that has never been matched.

Today, training and competing have become almost a science. At the Olympic Training Center in Colorado Springs, researchers study swimmers' strokes and conditioning in a swimming "treadmill" called the flume. It's the size of a very small pool. Water flows in and allows athletes to swim against the current while staying in one spot. Swimmers are videotaped, and their strokes are studied carefully so that they can make tiny improvements and shave precious seconds off their race times.

Swimming has been one of the United States' strongest Olympic events, and the Summer Games promise to be exciting. Be sure to watch the seven days of events to see if one of your favorite competitors gets the gold!

THE RACING COURSE

The long-course racing pool is 50 meters (that's about 55 yards). It has a minimum of eight lanes, each between seven and nine feet wide. The water is at least four feet deep, and its temperature must be between 78 and 80 degrees Fahrenheit. The front edge of the starting block is 30 inches above the surface. The flags at each end of the pool let backstrokers know when the wall is approaching. At the ends of every lane are electronic touch pads that automatically time every length and register the final race time to the hundredth of a second. The swimmers' times and places are posted electronically on a results board right after each event.

THE EVENTS

There are thirteen individual events for men and thirteen for women. There are also three relays for each. The events are listed below by stroke.

Freestyle

In the freestyle, the competitor picks the stroke. The most popular is the Australian crawl, which consists of alternating overhand motions combined with a flutter kick. In the shorter races—the 50-, 100-, and 200-meter—swimmers pour on the speed. Men can swim the 50-meter in as fast as twenty-one seconds, and women can do it in twenty-four seconds. A quick start is important, and in the 100- and 200-meter race, quick turns are vital, too.

The distance events—the 400-meter race and the 800-meter for women, and the 1500-meter for men—call for endurance. Swimmers spend hours learning how to maintain a steady pace. There are other strategies in distance swimming. When you watch these events, keep track of who leads in the beginning and who wins the race. It's not always the same swimmer! Some athletes like to swim the first half of the race more slowly and then catch up to the leaders near the end. The winners are those who are in the best shape and have mastered the art of pacing.

Backstroke

Men and women swim a 100-meter and a 200-meter backstroke. In this stroke, the swimmer stays on his or her back except during turns. The stroke calls for an alternating motion of the arms (a lot like the crawl stroke) with a flutter kick.

The flags above the pool signal to the swimmers that they are approaching the wall. Swimmers spend hundreds of hours perfecting their turns. They know exactly how many strokes it takes them to reach the wall from the flags. This helps them make turns without looking for the wall.

The start and the turn are critical in backstroke races. Be sure to note who makes the most of these important skills. New rules allow the swimmers to turn over on their stomachs during the turns. Some swimmers do an extended kick underwater off the wall. This takes practice with a professional coach.

Many backstrokers kick much harder at the end of the 200 than they do at the beginning. During the finish, you may notice some swimmers diving backward to touch the wall. This technique is a faster way to finish a backstroke race.

Breaststroke

The breaststroke may be one of the most difficult strokes to master. It requires simultaneous movements of the arms. The hands are pushed straight forward on or just under the surface of the water. Then the hands are pulled out, back, and together while the swimmer kicks to move forward. The timing of the arm movements and the kick is critical. The kick looks like a "frog" kick, with both legs coming around and down in a circular motion.

Breaststroke events call for the swimmer to touch the wall with both hands at the same time before executing the turn. Breaststrokers are allowed to take one complete stroke underwater off the start and the turn. To do this, the swimmer goes a little deeper underwater off the walls than in other strokes. See if you can tell which swimmers have the best underwater "pullouts." Something else you may notice is that some breaststrokers have stronger arms or legs. Usually the swimmers in the 100-meter races have stronger arm strokes, while those in the 200-meter races have stronger kicks.

Butterfly

Some experts consider the butterfly the most physically demanding stroke. It consists of simultaneous overhand strokes combined with a dolphin kick. In the dolphin kick, both legs move up and down together. If a swimmer in a butterfly event does a flutter kick, he or she is disqualified. Most "flyers" breathe with their head up, but some breathe by putting their head to the side. Butterfly swimmers must also touch the wall with both hands before turning.

The butterfly is the newest of the four strokes and was first swum in the 1956 Olympics. The distances for the butterfly are 100 meters and 200 meters. The 100 is a sprint, in which most swimmers breathe every two strokes. The 200 butterfly is one of the most grueling races. Many swimmers fade away in the last 15 to 25 meters of the race. The strongest finishers are those in the best physical shape, as well as the ones with the greatest mental toughness.

Many butterfly races are won or lost in the last two strokes. Those swimmers who end up a half stroke behind lose.

U.S. swimmer Mary T. Meagher (Madame Butterfly) still holds the world records she set in 1981 for the 100-meter (57.93 seconds) and the 200-meter (2:05.96 minutes).

Individual Medley

The I.M. features all four of the competitive strokes in one event. There are a 200 and a 400 I.M. In the 200 I.M., each swimmer does one length of each stroke, starting with the butterfly, then the back-stroke, then the breaststroke, and finally the freestyle. In the 400 I.M., each swimmer does two lengths of each stroke.

The most exciting part of watching the individual medley is observing how often the lead changes based on the swimmers' strong and weak strokes. The 400 I.M. is even more interesting because the lead can change many times. The strong butterflyers go out fast but often lag by the time the breaststroke comes. Watch especially closely during the breaststroke leg to see who catches up. Then it's usually an all-out race to the finish.

The 200-meter races usually end with a close finish; in the 400, there may be more distance between the finishers. Most experts consider the 400 I.M. the toughest race of all. The strategy usually is to swim the first 50 meters of each stroke smoothly and easily, then to push hard in the second length. The 400 event requires swimmers to be in great condition and competent in all four strokes.

Turns are very important in the I.M. Look to see which swimmers do a spin turn from the backstroke to the breaststroke.

Relays

There are two types of relays: freestyle and medley. In the freestyle relays, all four teammates swim freestyle. In the medley, each of the four swimmers from one team does a different stroke, starting with the backstroke, then the breaststroke, the butterfly, and the freestyle.

The critical factor in relays is the exchange: the part of the race in which one swimmer is finishing and the next is taking off. The best exchanges look as if the swimmer on the blocks leaves early, but they are really perfectly timed. The relay team practices exchanges hundreds of times. A plate on the starting block lets the officials know if a swimmer leaves the block before the incoming swimmer has touched the wall. If the swimmer on the block leaves early, the entire team is disqualified.

Relays are exciting because the lead changes depending on the strengths and weaknesses of each team. One team may appear to be in the lead, only to lose when a strong swimmer from another team begins his or her leg. Another reason for the excitement is that a country with no hope of winning individual medals can put four strong swimmers together for a medal-winning relay performance. The "team" part of the relay adds a lot of excitement, too. The person going last in a relay is called the anchor. Usually this person is the fastest swimmer. It's exciting to watch a team come from behind to win because of a fast anchor leg.

Don't miss the next exciting adventure of the

In Deep Water

American Gold Swimmers #4

Kristy Adams has her first crush on a boy—the handsomest brown-haired hottie she's ever seen! She's growing up, and her body is changing. It's all enough to make her want to stay home . . . forever!

Then Kristy learns that the boy she likes is also a swimmer—and he's on a rival team that the Surfside Waves are facing at an upcoming event. When she finds out that Jason thinks she's too competitive, Kristy has to decide what is more important: pleasing her very first boyfriend, or pleasing herself.